THE ANDERSON CHRONICLES
BOOK 4

NEFARIOUS INTENT

KIT KARSON

Book design by Bookery.design

ISBN 979-8-9900561-2-1 (hard cover)
ISBN 979-8-9900561-3-8 (paperback)
ISBN 979-8-9900561-4-5 (ebook)
ISBN 979-8-9900561-5-2 (audiobook)

FOR DON BALSER HIS GOLDEN INSIGHT

AND BRENT DOUCETT FOR
THE INSPIRATION

FOR NOTHING IS SECRET
THAT WILL NOT BE REVEALED,
NOR ANYTHING HIDDEN THAT WILL
NOT BE KNOWN AND COME TO LIGHT.

Luke 8:17

1

WHEN TREES AND grasses go dormant and creek waters freeze and the land is covered with a thick blanket of pure white snow, a different kind of magic fills the landscape of the Moonlight Mountains. Quiet peace descends as those creatures who are able retreat to warmer climates. Others choose cozy dens and a deep sleep, to be awakened only by the loving kiss of spring. Left are the hardier of the animal world. Tiny chickadees, enormous moose, and resilient humans exchange their summer frocks for thick winter coats, indifferent to winter's chill.

Feet on desk and head in hands, dreaming of white sand beaches and the warmth of the sun, Stone County Sheriff Peter Elliott barely caught himself from falling backward when his office door burst open, followed by a woman decked out in a full-length fur coat and matching hat. Sparkling diamond earrings peeked out from under a chic blonde bob. A stranger would have pegged her for a socialite stranded in a remote cow town. Peter knew better. Nancy May lived in the local senior apartments and spent her days drumming up excitement in an effort to stave off boredom.

"Peter! What are you doing sitting there? The light parade is tomorrow night and you missed dress rehearsal!"

Peter groaned. Every year while the rest of Anderson, Montana dusted off their Christmas decorations and practiced carols, Peter imagined ways to avoid the light parade. Tradition overruled personal preference and tradition demanded the sitting sheriff of Stone County lead the parade. On horseback. In full cowboy attire. The traditional outfit of wool and leather, handed down through many generations of sheriffs, reeked of the sweat of those past sheriffs and no amount of cleaning would diminish the odor. Peter would gladly pay for a new period designed costume, but was unanimously voted down by the parade committee. Tradition was tradition and for him to not wear the traditional outfit would bring bad luck . . . or something. Peter never did get a straight answer on that decision.

The clothing issue was a minor one. Peter could tolerate a musty outfit for a few hours once a year. What he objected to was the horse. He had no problem with horses in general. He had no issue with other people riding horses. Peter had issues with riding horses himself.

Decades earlier, as a young teen, Peter took a job on a local ranch. The sadistic owner of the ranch derived great pleasure in tormenting the young men who had the misfortune of finding themselves in his employ. Pegging Peter as an easy mark, the rancher picked a green-broke, young stallion from of his herd, saddled and bridled the skittish horse out of Peter's sight, and ordered Peter to mount and ride. Peter managed to get set in the saddle before the horse began to buck. He landed in a ditch across the road, miraculously intact. The horse turned tail and galloped into the next county. Peter handed in his spurs and swore he would never get on a horse again. Then he became sheriff.

"Can't you find someone else to lead the parade, Nancy?"

"Tradition is tradition, Peter. You have to do it." She dropped a worn blue duffel bag onto his desk. "If this is about the stinky clothes, I sprayed them with my best perfume this morning." She unzipped the bag. "Sniff. All you can smell is perfume."

Peter stifled a gag. "They smell like a hobo in a flower shop."

"Oh, don't be so picky. It's only for a couple hours. Besides, good news, Bert Smells has offered the use of a horse this year. A young and frisky one, not like that big lumbering thing you usually ride. Bert was so excited about you riding his new horse, he couldn't stop laughing."

"I'll bet." Bert Smells ran on the wrong side of the law on a regular basis and would be thrilled to see Peter lying in a ditch.

Peter thought fast. "Y'know, Nancy, I hate to disappoint Bert as excited as he is about the parade and all, but you know Seth Geary donates the horse every year. It's tradition, and tradition is tradition . . . besides, I promised him last year we would keep using his horse."

"You did? I wish you would have consulted me before making parade decisions. I am the committee chairwoman after all."

"I know, I know, but you were out of town or something and it slipped my mind."

"Well, okay. I'll break the news to Bert. He'll be so disappointed!"

Peter stood, gently took Nancy's arm, and led her toward the door.

"Are you sure you'll be ready for the parade?" she asked.

"I'll manage. It's the same route every year."

"But, I have a special surprise this year. Don't you want to know what it is?"

"Surprise me," said Peter as he led her through the outer office and to the door.

A shock of red hair lit up the work table along the back wall. Full of restless energy, Deputy Angus McLeod was sitting at a desk typing reports, which ranked high on his least favorite things to do, making him easily distracted. "Where'd Nancy get that fancy fur coat?" he asked.

Blond and buff, in his mid-twenties, office clerk Travis chuckled. "She scored it out of an old trunk she bought at a barn sale. They sold it cheap because the trunk was locked and they didn't have a key. Nancy wanted Peter to shoot it open."

"Did you?" asked Angus.

Peter rolled his eyes. "No, to Nancy's great disappointment, we managed to open it with a lock pick set. She was sure we'd find a skeleton and she'd have a cold case to solve. All she got was that fur coat and hat."

"Someone's treasure from a hundred years ago," mused Angus, whose mother collected a wide variety of antiques.

"So, how'd the trespassing call go?" asked Peter, pulling up a chair.

"Not so good for the snowmobilers."

"Do tell."

"Out-of-staters. Three half-drunk old men. They told Seth they got turned around and didn't realize they were on private property. He was pointing them in the right direction when he saw the cut fence."

"They actually cut his fence to go through?" asked Travis.

"Yep."

"What'd they cut the fence with?" asked Peter.

"Heavy duty wire cutters. One tripped in the snow getting off his machine to talk to Seth. The cutters fell out of his pocket. That's when Seth noticed the fence."

"So, they've done this before."

"Probably. When they realized they were caught, they hopped on their machines and took off the way they came. Seth called it in and told me which direction they were headed."

"Where'd you catch up with them?"

"The Black Pine trailhead parking lot. Seth met me there and ID'd them when they roared in."

"Get any resistance?"

"They tried to lie their way out of it. Said they found the fence that way, then accused Seth of framing them. When that didn't work, they sunk to 'the land belongs to everyone'."

"Where are they now?"

"Holding cells downstairs. I got tired of listening to them whine." Angus reached under the table and pulled out an evidence box. "Seth grabbed the wire cutters before they took off." He grinned. "Evidence."

"Good job. Too bad we can't make them repair the fence."

"Yeah, bummer for Seth. I don't blame him for closing off the trails to his land. It only takes a few hooligans like that to ruin it for everyone."

"Speaking of Seth," said Peter, "I need to chat with him about another matter.

2

THE GEARY PLACE, a working dairy farm, sat north of Anderson where hills retreated and the valley opened out on both sides of Flint Creek. Milking parlors and equipment sheds were tucked in hollows behind the surrounding hills, hidden from the roadside and beautiful valley vistas. The fertile fields of summer lay dormant under a blanket of snow and Flint Creek flowed under a layer of ice, giving the valley an air of emptiness.

Peter turned onto a familiar country lane. Over a hillcrest, in a hidden meadow, stood the Geary's rambling log house. Barns and stables filled a distant side yard. Evidence of children lay scattered in front of the house, up the steps, and onto a roomy covered porch. Sleds and lopsided snowmen took the place of the bikes and mud pies of summer.

Seeing a familiar vehicle parked in front of the barn and a light shining through the window, Peter drove past the house and parked next to Seth's truck.

"No worries about tracking snow in here," he said as he opened the door to the special kennel compartment in his Ford Explorer, freeing his German shepherd, Zack.

Outside, the barn spoke of new construction and modern times. Opening the door, Peter was met with mixed aromas of hay, horses, and mice, transporting him back in time to a long-forgotten barn of his childhood. He called out to announce his arrival.

"Hey, Seth. Are you in there?"

An Australian shepherd puppy, grown since Peter's last visit but just as wiggly, ran to greet him. Peter stooped to give her a scratch before she wiggled past to greet Zack.

"Hey, Peter," said Seth, wiping his hands on a rag as he walked out of the feed room. "You heard about my run-in with the snowmobilers today."

"Yeah, but that's not why I'm here."

"Oh?"

"Well, the light parade is tomorrow night."

Seth started to laugh. "I heard Bert Smells offered a wild stallion for you to ride this year."

"Good grief. Does nothing stay private in this town?"

"Not much. He was down at Dixie's Diner cheering your imminent demise."

"So . . . is Archie still alive?"

"He has a few more light parades in him."

Peter followed Seth down a line of stalls until they reached the final and largest stall in the corner of the barn. At the sound of their footsteps, a pair of nostrils poked out the open top half of the stall door, followed by the head of a golden-hued horse.

"Hi, Archie," said Peter, patting the big horse's nose.

"A gentle giant," said Seth. "I had the farrier out this morning. He gave Archie snowball pads and shoe studs. He's surefooted and ready for the parade."

Seth pulled a small apple out of his pocket and handed it to Peter. Peter held it under Archie's nose and smiled as he felt warm breath and soft horse lips against his hand. "I could almost like horses if they were all like Archie."

Seth's eyes twinkled. "You never did say, but I always wondered . . . was it Bert who put you on that wild horse when you were a kid?"

"Yeah, it was Bert. He straddles the fence when it comes to the law. When he crosses the line and I have to charge him, he accuses me of doing it out of spite because of the horse incident."

"Nothing is ever his fault, is it?"

"Not in his mind."

"Dixie called me this morning," said Seth, with a sideways glance at Peter.

"Oh?"

"It was after Bert was in the diner bragging about the wild horse. She was worried about you."

Peter felt a blush creep across his face, thinking about his childhood friend turned woman and their unfortunate first date. He cleared his throat. "I didn't think she wanted anything to do with me after I took her on that stakeout."

"Well, when your run-of-the-mill girl leaves a date cold, tired, and in need of a bathroom, she's likely to think twice about accepting another offer." He glanced at Peter. "Dixie's a step or two above run-of-the-mill. She understands. Give her a call."

3

RED AND GREEN Christmas lights danced on blue-tinged skin. That the couple was dead was obvious. Murder most likely. The method unclear. Zip ties held the wrists and ankles of the corpses tightly against rungs and spindles of bow back kitchen chairs. One chair lay tipped on its side, leaving its captive to endure a last moment of humiliation in a futile attempt to escape.

Stone County Sheriff's deputy, Tom Edwards, stood stunned, taking in the scene. Books and knickknacks swept clear of built-in wall shelves lay in jumbled piles. Slashed cushions from a tan corduroy couch cluttered the floor. *Was the killer looking for something or was this an act of rage?* thought Tom, as he set the cardboard box of groceries he was carrying on the glass top of a heavy wooden coffee table. He fumbled his cell phone while taking it out of a coat pocket, convincing himself it was the cold instead of nerves causing his fingers to shake. Rather than call dispatch, Tom called Sheriff Peter Elliott directly.

A thick slice of meat pizza hovered halfway to Peter's mouth as his phone chimed. He groaned. Setting the slice back in the box, he swiped his phone to answer. "Hey, Tom."

"Sorry to bother you, Peter. I know it's your pizza and football night, but . . . well, I thought you would want to know first."

Peter sighed. "What's going on? I didn't think you were on duty tonight."

"I'm not. I came to deliver groceries to the Celareses. You know, Frank and Alice."

"Older couple? Live in an old farmhouse up Saddleback Road?"

"Yeah. Them. Well . . . they're dead."

"Dead as in how?"

"Dead as in murdered."

"Oh boy."

"Yeah. What do you want me to do?"

"Sit tight. I'm on my way."

In Stone County, sheriff and coroner are dually elected, giving Peter the responsibility of both offices. A dead body required his presence regardless of the pizza and football situation. He disconnected with Tom and punched in the number for his nightshift dispatcher, Debbie Tonapah.

"Hey, Debbie," he said when she answered. "It's Peter. We have a murder scene on the mountain. At the home of Frank and Alice Celares. We need an ambulance for a transfer to the morgue. Two bodies."

"Oh, boy. Will do. Anything else?"

"Send Helen to process the crime scene. Oh, and give Dr. Hamm a heads up. He'll need to do the autopsies."

Peter disconnected, balanced his six-foot, five-inch and two hundred fifty pounds on an entryway chair, and pulled on winter boots, coat, and gloves. He slipped a cozy knit cap rather than the usual Stetson over his already unruly mahogany hair. The public, especially tourists, expected him to play the part of a western sheriff with cowboy hat and boots. After the first snow fall of the season, he was less inclined to appease that notion.

Zack lifted his satellite dish ears, yawned, and stretched on his bed in the corner. Not aggressive enough for the big city police force where he was trained, Zack redeemed himself in Anderson by sniffing out an occasional bad guy or victim.

"Sorry, Zack," said Peter, flipping him a doggy treat. "You have to stay here. Can't have your wet paws all over a crime scene and it's too cold for you to stay in the truck."

As an afterthought, Peter grabbed the pizza box on his way out the door.

THE DISTANCE WAS short as the bird flies, using a vehicle, not so much. Switchbacks, sharp curves, and a sheet of ice under a foot of fresh snow made driving treacherous on the winding mountain road leading to the Celareses' house. While most of Anderson rejoiced in the possibility of a white Christmas, Deputy Helen Ferguson cursed the snow that concealed evidence at a crime scene.

"It couldn't wait to snow until after the murder?" asked Helen as she climbed into Tom's truck where he was waiting with the heater running full blast.

Tom pushed a fur lined trapper hat further down onto his balding head and shivered. "It did. They've been in there for a while."

"So, no tracks when you drove up?"

"Nope. Whoever did this was long gone before the snow started."

When Peter pulled up next to them, Tom reluctantly turned off the motor and climbed out of the warmth of the truck. The thermometer registered a balmy twelve degrees Fahrenheit, but a biting wind blowing through the valley from the north set a windchill factor of negative four. Tom led the others to the back door of the house where Helen, the department crime scene expert, handed them each a set of waterproof boot covers. "We don't need our wet prints destroying evidence," she said, as she slipped covers over her own boots.

Protection donned, Tom led them into the house, through the kitchen, and to the ransacked living room where chair-bound bodies awaited investigation.

"I see why you were waiting in your truck," said Helen. "It's freezing in here."

"There's only a wood burning stove for heat. The fire was out and the back door hanging open when I got here," said Tom.

A thin flannel nightgown covered the frozen corpse of the female victim. Boxer shorts and bare legs peeked out of a plaid cotton robe on the male.

"Either ready for bed or just up for breakfast," commented Helen.

"Any sign of trauma?" asked Peter, as he studied glazed empty eyes and frosted blue skin.

"Not that I could see. My guess is they froze to death. The temperature's been in the low teens all day. It dipped below zero last night. Either way, it wouldn't take long," said Tom.

"How'd you happen to find them?" asked Helen

Tom pointed to the box of groceries sitting on the coffee table. "They called in an order last week and never came to pick it up. No answer on the phone. Judy got worried and asked me to check on them."

Tom owned the local grocery store. His wife, Judy, and grown children managed things so well that Tom rarely needed to be there. As a result, he spent his free time filling in as a deputy sheriff.

Peter took a pair of nitrile gloves out of his pocket and knelt next to Alice. He went through the motions of feeling for a pulse. Nothing. He examined each hand for self-defense wounds and broken nails. Red polish decorated with gold and silver Christmas designs covered each nail, all of them intact.

"Her right wrist is in a cast," said Peter. "Do you know anything about that?"

"She slipped and fell on the ice a while back. That's why she called in her grocery order. She couldn't drive and Frank is . . . was a horrible shopper."

"She sent him for pork chops and salad and he brought back beer and pretzels?"

"Something like that."

Moving on to Frank, Peter confirmed the lack of a pulse and studied the hands.

"The nails of a mechanic . . . packed with grease, but no sign of self-defense wounds here, either."

Seeing spots of blood on the floor, Peter shifted Frank's head. "There's an abrasion here," he said. "Probably caused when he tipped the chair over." He stood, removed his gloves, and shoved them into a pocket. "I'll need to notify next of kin."

"There's only the one son that I know of," said Tom. "Tony Celares. He's a loan officer at the bank."

"Yeah, I know him," said Peter, remembering all too well the kind man who tried to talk him out of buying the glorified shack he now called home.

"At least my camera lens won't fog up coming in from the cold," said Helen, shivering as she turned to retrieve the crime scene kit from her vehicle.

Boots thumped against the porch, signaling the arrival of the ambulance crew.

"That was quick," said Peter. He followed Helen out. She sent the crew back into the warmth of their vehicle, promising to call them in when the bodies were ready for removal.

Peter grabbed the pizza box out of his cab and handed it to Helen. "I'm heading back into town to notify the son. This'll keep you fed while you work the scene."

A bulky parka concealed Helen's burgeoning waistline and straining buttons. She grinned at the pizza box. Frigid weather at a murder scene was no time to worry about extra pounds. She needed sustenance to stay warm.

4

PETER PAUSED FOR a moment on the mountain and took in the warm glow of the town below. A fresh blanket of snow reflected and amplified thousands of Christmas lights making Anderson a beacon in the wilderness.

A pleasant view couldn't lighten Peter's mood. The image of the frozen couple troubled his mind, bringing with it memories of his own parents' murder decades past. He picked up his phone and called the sheriff's office.

"Hi," said Debbie. "Ambulance get there okay?"

"Yeah, thanks. Can you look up an address for Tony Celares?"

Debbie groaned. "Tony at the bank? The vics are related to him?"

"Yeah, his parents."

Debbie rattled off an address. "I don't envy you that job," she said.

Debbie previously held the odious position of secretary to Anderson's arrogant and incompetent Mayor Kalinski. Working in the sheriff's office, without question a more preferrable job, had its own unpleasant tasks.

Informing loved ones of a death is best handled in pairs. You never knew what sort of reaction you would get. Peter disconnected from Debbie and punched in the number for his older brother Paul, pastor of the local Baptist church.

"Hey," said Peter when Paul answered. "Are you busy?"

"No more than usual. Working on Sunday's sermon."

"Would you help me with a next of kin death notification?"

Paul audibly sighed. "Sure. Who's the deceased and who are we notifying?"

"Frank and Alice Celares deceased. Notifying their son Tony."

"Oh dear."

"You know them?"

"Frank and Alice are part of my flock."

"Not Tony?"

"Occasionally. You know, special occasions . . . Easter and Christmas."

Peter gave him Tony's address. "I'm on my way. Meet you there."

Born and raised in Stone County, Peter knew most folks by name or reputation, and the general location of every address. He drove without hesitation to Tony Celares's house, parked, waited for Paul, and braced himself for what was to come.

Paul pulled up behind Peter and joined him on the sidewalk. "How're you holding up?" he asked when Peter explained the situation.

Peter hesitated. "Fine, well. . . . not great, but I can't be sheriff and expect there'll never be a murder to deal with."

"Good enough."

A surprisingly elegant woman answered the door, too elegant for a dusty cow town like Anderson. She wore a well-fitting sheath dress in a sparkling red that accented her brown eyes and light blonde hair. Peter suspected she was on her way to a holiday party. She glanced at the men in annoyance.

"Sorry to disturb you," Peter said at her lack of greeting. "Is Mr. Celares home?"

"What is this about?"

"We need to speak with him on a personal matter."

She rolled her eyes and shut the door without asking them in. Peter stood stunned for a moment. He was used to hostility from criminals, not so much ordinary citizens.

The door soon reopened, this time by Tony Celares. He leaned against the frame, his right foot bare of shoe or sock held several inches above the floor. A pained expression creased his face.

"So sorry. Susan's upset with me. She has a tendency to take her anger out on anyone available."

He motioned them inside, turned, and hopped on one foot, using the wall as a crutch, into a living room carpeted in plush white.

Peter and Paul, in unison, hesitated and looked from the carpet to their boots.

"Don't worry about it," said Tony, waving them in. He lowered himself into an easy chair. "I told her white carpet was ridiculous, but she insisted. Apparently, it's all the rage in New York or somewhere."

Peter and Paul sank into a plush couch and watched as Tony wrapped a ziplock baggie of ice in a kitchen towel and held it against his big toe. They all jumped as the front door slammed, Susan leaving for the party.

"Susan's your wife?" asked Peter.

"Yeah, my wife. This is why she's mad tonight," he said, pointing to his toe. "My gout flared up and I refused to drag myself to the country club Christmas gala. It's the highlight of her social calendar." He groaned and lowered his leg onto the footrest, gently laying his foot on a pillow. "No way I can dance the night away with this toe." He glanced up and grinned. "I would take this pain any day to get out of hobnobbing with the rich and famous."

"How many rich and famous folks do we have in Anderson?" asked Paul in all seriousness.

"None. Nada. Zilch," answered Tony. "Just a lot of wannabees. Unfortunately, my wife is one of them."

"Is she from around here?" asked Peter.

"No. I met her in college back east. I majored in finance. She thought I was going to be a high rolling investment banker. Boy was she surprised when we unloaded the U-Haul in Anderson."

"How long have you been married?"

"Thirty-two years in May. You're wondering why she stuck around?"

"Uh . . . yeah."

"Out of pride. She would never admit she was wrong." He adjusted his ice pack.

"No kids?" asked Paul.

"No kids. She never conceived. I don't know if it was on purpose or if one of us is infertile. She never pushed it. Easier to play 'lady of the manor' if she's not driving a minivan or pushing a stroller."

Peter cleared his throat to change the subject and Tony reached to pull his wallet out of a back pocket. "Is cash okay or do you want a check?"

"Uh . . . what do you mean?"

"You're here collecting for a community charity, aren't you?"

"Uh . . .no. We're here on official business."

For the first time since they walked in, Tony looked worried. "The sheriff and the pastor?"

Peter cleared his throat. "It's your parents. One of our deputies found them."

Reality dawning, Tony said, "Found them . . . you mean—"

"Tom Edwards went to the house to bring them groceries. They were deceased."

The color drained from Tony's usually florid face. "I . . . I don't understand. I talked to them, well, a couple of days ago." He rubbed his temples. "Both of them? How could that be?"

"We believe they were murdered."

Any ability to speak left Tony, replaced with open-mouthed shock.

Paul rose and laid his hand on Tony's shoulder for comfort while Peter described, with restraint, the scene on the mountain.

Tears filled Tony's eyes. "I've been so busy . . . I haven't been taking care of them like I should."

"We need you to identify the bodies," said Peter as he stood to go. "There has to be an official ID before Dr. Hamm can perform the autopsy."

In shock, Tony sputtered, "W . . . where do I go? Susan. I need Susan."

"I can take you to the morgue," said Peter. "The ambulance is on the way there." He gave Paul a questioning glance.

"I can pick up Susan," offered Paul. "Did you say she was at the country club?"

Tony nodded and studied his swollen toe in confusion, unable to process a solution.

"Do you have boots to fit around that toe?" asked Paul, giving Tony's shoulder a gentle squeeze.

"Uh . . . yeah." He pointed to the entryway. "By the door. Black. Probably still wet."

Peter, long past worrying about muddying the carpet, found the boots and brought them into the living room. He helped Tony ease a boot over his toe and both men helped him to his feet, out the door, and into Peter's Ford Explorer.

"I'll find Susan and meet you at the morgue," said Paul as he waded through knee deep snow to his own vehicle.

THE BLANDNESS OF the country club meeting room was barely disguised with dim lights and a profusion of multicolored garland.

"What do you mean they're dead?" demanded Susan, much too loudly, after Paul lead her to the edge of the room to break the news.

Paul explained, "Tony is at the morgue identifying the bodies. He asked me to find you and bring you there."

Susan looked around the room in dismay. "But . . . but, I'm supposed to hand out the white elephant gifts."

Accustomed to inappropriate reactions in times of stress, Paul said, "I'm sure we can find someone else to hand out the gifts. Tony needs you."

"What about my car? I can't leave my car."

"I'll drop you back here to pick it up afterwards."

Not giving her opportunity for more excuses, he took her arm and guided her through the throng of curious onlookers, all dressed for a New York gala.

5

ODIES PROCESSED AND loaded, Tom glanced at Helen. "How are we going to split the search?" he asked.

"We can flip for it," said Helen, digging into her pocket for a coin. "Loser gets outside."

"Fair enough," said Tom. He hated the coin toss. He invariably lost.

Helen flipped the coin into the air, but held her hand on her arm, covering the result. "Call it."

"Tails."

Helen lifted her hand and felt a twinge of guilt. "Heads."

After Tom left, she studied the trashed living room. That the perpetrator was looking for something didn't make sense. What could possibly be hidden in the jumble of broken knickknacks? Important papers folded into the pages of a paperback novel seemed a bit too cliché. The slashed couch cushions? No, this was an act of rage.

Helen ignored the mess and wandered into the kitchen. A cast iron frying pan held the remnants of bacon grease. On the table, egg yolk oozed in frozen rivulets next to half-eaten toast halves. A breakfast interrupted. Unlike the living room, the kitchen held no sign of a disturbance.

Beyond the kitchen, a stairway led to a second story. The first room, a bedroom converted into a multi-purpose room, held a sewing machine on a sturdy table in one corner, and an L-shaped computer desk and hutch in another. Next to the desk stood a two-drawer file cabinet. Like the shelves in the living room, these drawers were open and the contents removed. Unlike the chaos of the living room, the papers from the filing cabinet sat in neat piles on the floor. *Looking for something,* thought Helen. On the desk, a password book lay open. Precise printing recorded every password and username required for every website Frank and Alice Celares used, starting with the password to log into the computer. Bank accounts. Credit cards. Computer files. Helen sighed. She dusted the password book and the computer keys for fingerprints and packed them into an evidence box along with the piles of papers from the file cabinet.

Continuing down the hallway, Helen found a tidy bathroom. Tooth brushes stood untouched in a cup and the medicine cabinet remained intact. The next bedroom, Helen guessed, belonged to the Celareses. The unmade bed could be explained. Frank and Alice were in their pajamas. Housework would come after breakfast. The ransacked closet felt more like the search Helen found with the file cabinet. Clothing remained on hangers, but everything from the bottom of the closet and the overhead shelf lay in the middle of the floor. Shoe boxes were emptied and then tossed aside. Photo albums, once stacked neatly in a cardboard box, lay in a pile. Helen dusted for fingerprints on each box and cursed the mud-brown frieze carpeting that hid both dirt and footprints. She reminded herself that the murders happened before the snow, but after the freeze. *Perfect weather for a murderer,* she thought. *No footprints, wet or dirty.*

"Hey," said Tom from the doorway, making her jump. "Did you find anything?"

"A computer and book of passwords. How about you?"

"Typical junk in the shed; old furniture and rusty bikes. The barn is cool . . . like the rancher walked out a hundred years ago and hasn't been back. Farm equipment, a wagon, harnesses, and saddles. There's even a forge in back where they did their own blacksmithing."

"There'll be a lot of happy collectors when all that goes to auction."

"Yep. Are we about done? It's way past my dinnertime."

Helen stood and stretched. "Sure. Let's take a peek in this last room."

Once belonging to Tony Celares, the boy, the last bedroom held an air of dust and neglect. Faded posters covered the walls and dozens of trophies lined shelves along the top. The closet door hung open, everything removed. This time, overturned plastic bins of building blocks and piles of comic books littered the floor.

Tom squinted up at the trophies. "Little league, spelling bees, and bowling," he commented. "Our Tony was quite the bowler."

Helen laughed. "I don't remember that but I didn't hang out at the bowling alley myself."

Tom looked surprised. In his mid-forties, sometimes he forgot that Helen was at least ten years older. "You went to school with Tony?"

"He's a few years older than me."

"Did you know him well?"

"Not so much. I mostly remember that his dad was the school bus driver."

Investigation complete for the time being, Tom and Helen stopped and grabbed the computer and files. They tromped down the stairs and out the door, engaging the lock before they left.

"Tony will have a key," said Helen. "We don't need nosy Nellies up here going through things."

6

MOST STREETS IN Anderson consisted of dirt, mud, or packed ice and snow depending on the season. Main Street, the only one approved for paving by the town council as a concession to the tourist trade, branched off from the highway at the bottom of the valley. A typical mishmash of buildings lined the street as it followed the rises and dips of foothills leading into the pine-covered slopes of the Moonlight Mountains. Original miners' log cabins stood next to shabby nineteenth century brick homes. Decaying barns teetered into crumbling foundations. Up the hill and around a curve, the town transformed into a tourist haven. Colorfully painted late Victorian era houses dressed in towers and turrets rubbed shoulders with stately red brick professional buildings.

Treasure hunters flocking to Anderson for rare Montana sapphires stayed to enjoy the many other attractions. To the south, Empire Peak, etched with ski runs, brought enthusiasts in the winter months. Flint Creek, flowing north and west, lured fly fishermen during the summer. Tourists flocked to the brewery year-round. High-end local artisans, a candy store, souvenir T-shirts, and ice cream entertained the rest.

The morning after the bodies were found, the cold spell having broken during the night, Peter left his cozy bungalow and walked several blocks of snow-covered road to the stately brick and granite courthouse occupying the highest point of town proper. At the back door, he cleaned balls of ice from between Zack's toes and brushed snow from his fur.

"Can't have you melting all over the place."

They took the stairs to the second floor and down the hall to the sheriff's office. Inside, they found Tom and Helen belly up to a box of donuts. Travis smiled indulgently. He considered donuts an important part of his office clerk duties and made sure to have fresh ones on hand each morning for the deputies.

"How'd it go at the Celareses?" asked Peter.

"It was touch and go getting them into the body bags the way they were frozen sitting up like that," said Tom around a mouthful of maple long john.

"One on the gurney and the other on a backboard on the floor," added Helen, powdered sugar coating the front of her uniform shirt and sifting into the gaps between buttons. "It worked. How'd Tony take the news?"

"He was in shock, but we got the ID. Dr. Hamm said the bodies had to thaw out in the morgue fridge for at least a week and he would get back to us." Peter grabbed his favorite chocolate cream-filled out of the donut box, broke off a piece and tossed it to Zack before he took a bite himself.

"A whole week?" asked Travis.

"Yeah, something about thawing evenly so the outer parts don't rot while the inner parts are still frozen."

Travis, not a fan of gore, stifled a gag.

"I'm betting they froze to death," said Tom.

"Me too," agreed Helen. "But, stomach contents could give us a clue about time of death."

"Speaking of clues," said Peter. "Did you find any on site?"

"Not much," said Helen. "We brought back the home computer and papers from a file cabinet. Clem said she would come over today and work on fingerprints."

Retired rancher and forensics enthusiast, Clementine Cordelia Smith hung up her saddle and spurs when her husband died. After acquiring a degree, she replaced ranching with forensics, vowing to use her education, money, and free time supporting the Anderson Sheriff's Department. As a result, Stone County had forensic equipment and capabilities far exceeding a typical rural sheriff's department.

"Lots of prints?" asked Peter.

"As many as you would expect in a house that hadn't been wiped clean. My guess is whoever tied Frank and Alice to those chairs and ransacked their living room was wearing gloves."

"Anything else?" asked Peter.

"This all went down after the last freeze and before the snowfall, so no muddy tracks. Also, no note from the perp saying, 'I did this and here's my contact information.'"

"So, we have the usual murder with no clues situation."

"Yep."

"Great. Does anyone know anything about this couple? Any rumors floating around town that would suggest an imminent murder?"

"Another murder?" asked a voice.

"Birdie!" chimed the group in unison as they turned and found Deputy Birdie Bradshaw standing in the doorway.

"How's the wrist?" asked Travis. "All healed up?"

Birdie, with ebony hair in a pixie cut and the bone structure to pull it off, could pass for a runway model even in her deputy uniform. She waved her right hand in the air showing off a bare wrist. "Just saw Dr. Hamm. He removed the cast and cleared me for duty." She walked into the room and handed Peter her medical release.

"Does this mean I'm off night shift?" asked Helen, hopefully.

Birdie looked at Peter. She wasn't sure where she stood after being imprisoned and hurt during the last murder investigation.

"You've been cleared of any wrongdoing," said Peter. He didn't have to tell her to keep dispatch apprised of her location in the future. She learned that lesson the hard way.

Birdie breathed a sigh of relief. "So, what's this about a murder?"

"Two, actually," said Travis, who couldn't hide his delight at Birdie's return.

"A couple living on the mountain. Tom found them frozen to death in their house yesterday," explained Peter.

"How is that a murder?"

"They were strapped to kitchen chairs with zip ties. The fire was out and the door left hanging open."

"There were no signs of defensive wounds on either of the victims," said Peter. "Fingernails were intact. There was no sign of a struggle anywhere in the house. From the scene, it looks like Frank and Alice were interrupted in the middle of breakfast. Why would they quietly move their chairs into the living room and allow themselves to be zip tied?"

"Because the perp had a gun," offered Helen.

"Exactly. So why didn't he shoot them instead of leaving them to slowly freeze to death?"

"Two reasons I can think of," said Tom. "One, he didn't want anyone to hear the gunshots. That doesn't fly, though. They don't have any close neighbors and nobody around here would think twice about hearing gunshots outside city limits. Two, he wanted them to suffer."

"Or she," said Helen. "A woman with a gun is as powerful as a man."

"True," said Tom. "Which brings us back to motive. Do you think that bus accident last fall could have anything to do with this?"

"What bus accident?" asked Birdie, an Eastern Montana native who recently signed on with the department. "I'm out of touch. I've spent the last two months in Miles City with my parents." She glanced around the room sheepishly. "Mom and Dad were so upset about what happened, they waited on me hand and foot."

"Frank Celares drove bus for the school," said Tom. "Mostly for the sports teams, but he filled in for the regular school bus route now and then." Tom took a bite of his donut, chewed, and swallowed before he continued, "Last fall he took the football team to a game in Frenchtown." Tom looked down, unable to continue.

Helen picked up the story. "On the way home, the bus went off the road. Three students died." She glanced over at Tom. "One of the boys was Tom's nephew."

Tom cleared his throat and wiped tears away with the back of his hand.

"He has a point," said Travis. "The parents of those boys blamed Frank. He was forced to resign."

"For good reason. Rumors around town said he was drunk as a skunk," said Tom. "Parents put so much pressure on the school, it wasn't worth hanging on to a part-time bus driver."

"If he was drunk, was he charged for those deaths?" asked Birdie.

"The accident happened in Missoula County so I didn't see the report, but as far as I know, no charges were filed," said Peter. "Nick Patterson is the sheriff over there. I'll give him a call and see what I can find out. Helen, work on processing those files from the house. Look for anything that might point to a murder motive . . . threatening letters, that sort of thing. Travis can work on searching through the computer."

"On it, Boss," they said in unison.

"Where's Angus?" asked Peter.

"Domestic over at the Sluice Box trailer court," said Travis.

"Not surprising. With this cold spell, everyone's been shut up at home too long getting on each other's nerves."

"Ain't that the truth."

"Get a list together of those boys from the accident, parents' names and addresses," said Peter. "When Angus gets back, I need to talk with him."

"Sure, Boss."

Peter frowned. "Tom . . . in my office."

Surprised by Peter's uncharacteristic gruffness, Tom hesitated for a moment before he stood and followed. He waited next to a leather chair facing Peter's desk and studied the vintage western art covering the walls. Usually a cozy, welcoming space, today the air was filled with tension.

"Sit down," said Peter with a sigh. "We need to talk."

Tom relaxed and sunk into the chair. "What's going on?"

"You're off the case, Tom. I need you to turn in your badge and gun until further notice."

Tom's face flushed with embarrassment. "What? But, why? Did I do something wrong?"

"You found the murder victims and people will assume you have a grudge against Frank Celares because of your nephew. That makes you a suspect."

"What?! You don't actually think I had anything to do with those murders!"

"What I think doesn't matter. You know as well as I do that Mayor Kalinski will latch on to anything he can to find fault with this department. He'll have everyone in town accusing me of covering for you. The best thing for both of us is for you to lie low for a while . . . but don't leave town. We'd never hear the end of that one."

"Yeah, you're right," said Tom, appeased. "What's his problem, anyway?"

Peter shrugged. "The sheriff's office is one of the few departments he has no control over. Besides, he hasn't forgiven us for giving Debbie the night dispatch job."

Tom laughed. "Okay, I'll hang out at the store and annoy Judy until things settle down."

"Oh, and Tom . . ."

"Yeah?"

"Don't be offended if one of us comes around asking for your alibi."

After Tom left, Peter punched in the number for the Missoula County Sheriff's Office.

"Sheriff Patterson," said a weary voice.

"Hey, Nick, you sound like you've had a rough day."

"Peter! Good to hear from you . . . as long as you don't have a complaint."

"No complaint," said Peter. "What's going on in Missoula County that has you frazzled?"

He heard a deep sigh on the other end of the line.

"Someone decided it was a good idea to combine the Christmas stroll with a renaissance fair. Someone else decided it was a good idea to give out free samples of hot spiced mead. Homemade, of course. If I had to guess, the alcohol content in that stuff is through the roof. Add a bunch of guys running around with pretend swords and women dressed like medieval barmaids, mix them up with cowboys in town doing their Christmas shopping and the local hipsters . . . well, you can just imagine."

Catching his breath from laughing, Peter said, "Jail full?"

"We confiscated the mead and roped off a tent at the fairgrounds for the drunks. When they can pass a breathalyzer, they get their keys back and we'll send them home with a warning."

"Gee, my murder case is sounding dull."

"Another murder?! Good grief, you're going to beat Missoula County in murder stats at this rate."

"Definitely not a contest I want to win."

"Is that why you're calling. Is your murder connected to us?"

"Indirectly. Possibly. What can you tell me about that bus accident that happened a couple months ago? The one that killed three basketball players."

"Black ice on a curve. There were several accidents in the area that day."

"So, no fault found with the driver? Speed? Alcohol? Anything?"

"Nope. Oh, we tested him for drugs and alcohol. He came back clean. There was no indication he was speeding or distracted. No cell phone activity."

"So, just bad roads and bad luck?"

"Yep."

"Thanks, Nick. That's all I needed to know."

"How is that accident connected to your murder case?"

"The bus driver and his wife are the victims. We thought the accident might be linked to motive."

"Aahhh. Well, good luck with that."

"Yeah, and good luck with your drunken brawl." Peter rang off, rested his heels on his desk, and leaned back in his chair to think.

Angus poked his head in the door. "You wanted to see me?"

"Yeah, have a seat." Peter lowered his feet to the floor and filled Angus in on the Celareses' murders and the link to the bus accident. "According to Nick Patterson, it was a no-fault accident. Frank Celares was cleared of any wrongdoing. Travis has a name and address list of the boys and their parents. I want you to interview them . . . get a feel for their state of mind . . . whether any of them are angry enough about the accident to commit murder."

7

ORIGINALLY A HOMESTEAD, split first by the addition of the state highway and then as the result of several family feuds, the remaining twenty acres struggled along as a hobby farm. In warmer months, hundreds of chickens scattered hither and yon across the acreage, foraging bugs and greens. Several pygmy goats and a pair of woolly llamas filled in the bare spots, all watched over by a mismatched pack of dogs.

Frigid days kept the animals inside shelters and left the farm with an air of abandonment. Sadness overwhelmed Angus as he drove into the yard, knowing of the loss of a son. As he parked next to a rusted and worn farm truck, a barking mass of fur-covered mongrels barreled out of the house and surrounded his vehicle. Angus felt a trickle of cold sweat trail down his back. His stomach clenched. An attack by a vicious pit bull during a previous investigation left Angus with a very rational fear of dogs. He breathed a sigh of relief when a tiny woman wearing an odd assortment of multicolored ponchos over jeans and muck boots banged through the screen door.

"Knock it off, you knuckleheads!" she hollered in a voice deeper than would be expected.

Tail wags replaced barks as the mob turned to greet their master.

"They're harmless," said the woman, as she approached Angus's now open window. "What brings you clear out here? My fussy neighbors couldn't possibly be complaining about the chickens. They've been hunkered down in the coop since this cold spell hit."

Angus recognized the woman from her booth at the Anderson farmers' market where she sold free range chicken eggs and knit clothing items she advertised as Montana Llama Originals. His list of the parents of bus accident victims had her down as Ms. Angela Brown, mother of deceased son, Asher. The brown hair held more gray and the face deeper lines than he remembered from the months before the accident.

"No, Ms. Brown," he said. "We haven't had any complaints, but I'd like to come in and talk about a few things."

"Uh . . . sure," she said, wary. The last time a sheriff's deputy showed up at her door for something other than a neighbor's complaint, she learned of her son's death.

Angela whistled to the dogs and turned toward the house, allowing Angus to follow, or not. His choice.

Angus cracked the vehicle door open, watching for a change of mood in the dogs who were now following their master. Nothing. He stepped out and closed the door behind him. A few dogs glanced in his direction, but tails continued to wag so Angus swallowed his fear and joined the procession into the house.

Inside, Angus hesitated. Winter, known as mud and wet season, played havoc on indoor floors. Custom varied depending on the household. Some folks required footwear to be taken off upon entering, others chose cleaning floors over the bother of removing boots.

Angela glanced back at Angus. "Close the door and come in. You can't make the floor any dirtier than it already is with these dogs running in and out." She led him into a spacious kitchen warmed by a wood burning stove and motioned toward the table. "Have a seat. Coffee or tea?"

"Coffee, thanks."

"Me too. I wouldn't ask, but that sheriff of yours always wants tea. I thought all you coppers drank bad coffee."

"Uh, yeah, Peter's not into coffee."

Angela set a mug in front of Angus and filled it with steaming coffee from a carafe. She poured another mug for herself, set the carafe back on its warmer plate, and sat at the table across from Angus.

Not one for small talk, Angus dove in. "It must be hard to keep up with things around here since your son died."

Coffee splattered across the table as Angela dropped her cup mid-sip. The cup bounced off the table, shattering as it hit the floor. She leaped from her chair with a curse, grabbed a roll of paper towels from the counter, and began sopping up the mess. Angus grabbed paper towels, catching the drips on the floor and pushing pieces of broken cup into a pile. On a whim, he pocketed the cup handle.

Finished with the table, Angela brought a broom over and began sweeping the cup fragments into a dustpan.

"Is that why you're here? All this time and not a one of you has come to ask me about the accident."

Angus felt a twinge of guilt. Growing up on a remote ranch with no one but his twin sister, Char, and an assortment of animals to talk to hadn't taught him the finer points of polite conversation. He knew by Angela's reaction that his approach lacked tact. Watching as she dumped the cup remnants into a waste basket and put away the broom, he struggled to find the right words to mend the conversation.

"I'm sorry I upset you," said Angus. "I can be blunt sometimes."

Surprised by the sudden gentleness, Angela gave Angus a weak smile. "S'okay. It's not an easy subject."

"Are you okay to answer a few questions?"

"Might as well get it over with. What d'ya need to know?" Angela collected the wet paper towels and tossed them into the waste basket.

"Tell me what you know about the accident."

"Everyone in town knows that bus driver was drunk. They let him run around free as a bird while Asher . . . Asher, my sweet boy . . ." She dropped to her chair, put her head in her hands, and sobbed.

Angus sat full of guilt for putting a mother through this pain. He waited as several minutes passed. Tears spent, Angela sat up and wiped her face with a paper towel.

"What makes you think the bus driver was drunk?" asked Angus.

"Everyone knows. People saw him drinking. They told me."

"You weren't at the game?"

"No. I should have been there, but there was a craft fair in Missoula that day." She glanced at Angus. "Craft fairs bring in a big chunk of our income and Missoula is one of the biggest. I couldn't afford to miss it."

"So, you didn't personally see the bus driver drinking?"

"Uh . . . no, people told me."

Angus pulled a notebook and pencil out of his pocket. "Who told you the bus driver was drinking? Do you have names of these witnesses?"

"Uh . . . just people around town. I don't remember exactly who."

"Do you know the bus driver," Angus glanced at his notes, "Frank Celares?"

"Of course, I know who he is. It's a small town and he's been driving the bus for years."

"Not anymore. He was fired after the accident."

Angela raised her voice in frustration. "He got off easy. He deserves to be dead instead of those kids."

Several heads lifted from the pile of mutts in front of the fire. Angus braced himself for an attack when he heard a growl.

"Did you know the Missoula County Sheriff's Office investigated? Frank Celares was cleared of any wrongdoing. Alcohol and drug tests were negative. A patch of black ice caused the accident."

Shocked into silence, Angela sat with her mouth open. "That can't be. Everyone says he was drunk."

"Small town gossip can ruin someone's life . . . or take someone's life. Frank Celares is dead. We're investigating his murder," explained Angus.

Angela sat speechless for a moment, processing the information. She asked, "Why are you here?"

"We're questioning anyone who might have a grudge against Frank because of the accident."

"What?! He murders my son and now I'm being investigated?"

Torn between compassion for a grieving mother and the obligation to question a suspect, Angus swallowed his emotions. "I understand that this is difficult for you, but I have to ask these questions."

"Whatever. Just get it over with."

"Can your account for your whereabouts yesterday?" Angus studied her face as she answered, looking for signs of deception.

She hesitated in thought, "I haven't left the place for days. It's been cold and miserable, and I don't have a reason to go anywhere."

Angus considered the trail of tire tracks he followed from the highway to the house. "Have you had any visitors? Anyone who can vouch for you being here?"

"No. I live alone since Asher died." Nervous, she stood abruptly and walked to the door. "I would like you to leave now."

Angus considered the lie and chose to let it pass for the moment. He closed his notebook and slipped it and the pencil back into his pocket. "Thank you for your time. We may have more questions in the future," he said as he stood to leave, thankful the mutt pack stayed in next to the fire.

8

IN THE EARLY days, Anderson, Montana existed to serve ranchers and then miners. While ranchers valued the abundance of grass and water above ground, miners dug into the earth for their treasures. The town took root and thrived around an array of sloping hills, steep gullies, and exposed banks of gravel caused by endless seasons of snowfall, heaving frost, spring thaws, and human excavation. As Anderson grew, streets were formed, not in a carefully planned grid but winding and weaving across the most passable routes.

Behind Main Street, a section of particularly rough terrain resulted in a rabbit warren of dead ends and narrow alleys inhabited by the seedier elements of Anderson society. Rumors of an underground network of escape tunnels and drug dens filtered through the gossip mill. Townsfolk called this area The Burrow and decent folk had no reason to wander in that direction.

On Angus's list of deceased boys, an address and the word 'burrow' filled in the area after the name of the second boy. By design, most signage in The Burrow had been removed and houses were without numbers. Residents preferred not to be found, especially by law enforcement. Without an organized street map to follow, and minimal signage, an address wasn't much help. Angus's only choice was to begin on the outskirts of The Burrow and work his way in.

He made a point of phoning Travis first to report his location. "If you don't hear from me by the end of the day, send in a search party."

"Sure," laughed Travis. "Although chances are they'll toss your body into one of those secret tunnels I've heard about."

Angus drove slowly over roads rutted with ice and snow. Studying neglected shacks surrounded by mounds of snow-covered litter and rusted-out car frames, he saw the first sign of life and decided to take a chance. He pulled up to the curb and got out of his vehicle.

"Whatever yer lookin' fer, I saw nuthin,' know nothin','" hollered a thin, greasy man from a sagging front porch.

Typical, thought Angus. Wading through fresh powdery snow, he kicked up crushed beer cans in varying stages of decay and considered the date of his last tetanus shot. He climbed a short flight of rickety steps and sat, uninvited, on a chair next to the man.

Still smarting from his faux pas with Angela Brown, Angus hesitated before saying, "I'm looking for June Revell and Doug Kromer. Parents of Carl Revell."

"What you wanna be botherin' those folks for?"

"We're investigating the bus accident that killed Carl," fibbed Angus. "I need to ask them a few questions."

The man, eyes narrowed, studied Angus. "You wanna' beer?"

Sensing a test, Angus hesitated. On duty meant no alcohol, but one beer with the guy could be the key to information. Peter would understand. "Sure."

Grinning, the man stood and held out his hand. "Vern Clark. At least that's the name I use in polite company."

Angus took his hand, surprised at the firm grip and thick callouses. "Good to meet you, Vern. Angus McLeod."

"Oh, I know who ya' are. We keep track 'a coppers, ifn' ya' know what a' mean."

Angus didn't know, but any reasons that came to mind weren't pleasant. He was relieved when the can of beer arrived unopened. *At least he's not planning to poison me and hide my body in a tunnel.*

The beer was as cold as the weather, and Angus shivered, but made an effort at chit chat. "You have the hands of a working man, Vern. What do you do when you're not at home?"

"Odds an' ends. Build stuff. Roofing. Whatever keeps the beer fridge full."

"So, you get around . . . talk to people. What do you hear about that bus accident?"

"Not much. Stuff happens." Vern took a long swig of his beer, emptying the can and tossing it into the front yard where it disappeared into a snowbank.

"I'd sure like to hear his parents' take on the whole thing," said Angus.

Vern popped the top on another beer. "Her kid. Doug never claimed him as far as I know." He took a swig and considered. Burrow protocol frowned on giving addresses to law enforcement. "Wouldn't do you no good. That kid hasn't been around here for a coupla' years."

"This was the address the school gave."

"Official address maybe. He hooked up with that basketball team and got all high an' mighty. Told Doug an' Juney they couldn't have alcohol in the house. No more parties cuz he needed his beauty sleep 'ah reckon'," Vern shook his head. "Can't tell about kids these days. No appreciation."

"They kick him out?"

"Yep. Told him to find someplace that'd suit his new, higher standards."

"You think they might know anything about the accident?"

"Yeah, but they ain't home. Ifn' ya don't tell them where ya heard, I'll send ya in their direction."

"Fair enough."

"Check the Roost. Some kinda' pool tournament goin' on."

"Thanks. I appreciate it." Angus finished his beer, crushed the can, and tossed it onto a pile on his way back to his vehicle. *When in Rome and all that.*

⸻ ❖❖❖ ⸻

ORIGINALLY A HOLE-IN-THE wall hangout for cattle rustlers, Rustler's Roost wore its name like a badge of honor. Most modern-day cattle rustlers kept a low profile, but the Roost remained a hangout for every other kind of dirtbag. Worries of his body being dumped into the infamous cellar of the Roost replaced Angus's fear of the tunnels underneath The Burrow. Standing on the rustic boardwalk facing the Roost, Angus punched in the number for the sheriff's office.

"Hey, Travis," said Angus when the phone was answered. "I'm done at The Burrow and going into the Roost."

"Glad you made it out. Personally, I always thought the tunnels under The Burrow would be a better option than that creepy cellar at the Roost."

"Ha ha. This shouldn't take more than a half hour or so."

"I'll keep close to the phone."

Anticipating dim lighting and a haze of smoke, Angus closed his eyes for a few seconds before he opened the door. Walking through brought him back to a time of robbers and rustlers and outlaw dens. His steps echoed on wood plank floors, no longer covered in the sawdust of early days. The original rough-hewn bar still stood; unique carvings added through the years by bored patrons with sharp pocket knives. No longer required to stand with only a footrail for support, bellying up to the bar meant relaxing on a comfortable modern barstool. Rough shelves behind the bar held bottles of booze, no sissified fancy mirror or ornately carved wood like the respectable saloons.

Angus found Mary, Roost owner and sometimes friend to the sheriff's office, sitting at the end of the bar. Mary, with a hawklike nose, dark beady close-set eyes, and a receding chin, had never been considered attractive. A lifetime of smoking and drinking carved lines into her face beyond normal aging. In spite of this, Mary retained a certain air of dignity that years of rough living couldn't diminish. Angus found her nursing a cigarette and sipping from an old-fashioned glass filled with an amber liquid.

"Whiskey?" asked Angus. "I thought you were off the stuff after that stint in the hospital."

"Made me too nervous," said Mary. "I kept imagining I was going into DTs. Nope, better to stay on the stuff than risk another coma. I keep a bottle on me whenever I go out now. Just in case."

"Isn't it whiskey that put you in the coma?" asked Angus. He shook his head, baffled at the skewed logic of an addict. "Never mind. I came looking for June Revell and Doug Kromer. Are they in here?"

Eyes narrowed, Mary asked, "What do you need them for?"

"I'm investigating the bus accident that killed their son."

"That was months ago."

"I know. I wanted to get their take on the whole thing."

Mary pointed her nose toward the back of the room where a crowd gathered around several pool tables. "They're back there somewhere."

Angus studied the crowd. "Could you give me a hint?"

Mary took a drag on her cigarette and washed it down with a swig of whiskey. "They have tattoos and they're wearing blue jeans." Her laughter ended in a fit of coughing.

"That would cover everyone back there."

"Okay, but you didn't hear it from me. They're on the team wearing the red shirts. Doug has on that stupid fox tail hat and June's hair is dyed purple. She's wearing lipstick to match. You can't miss them."

"Thanks, Mary. I appreciate it." He turned toward the crowd and then looked back at Mary. "If you ever want help kicking either of those habits, we can get you into a program."

Mary nodded and tapped her glass on the bar for a refill.

9

"I'VE EXAMINED THE bodies from head to toe," said Dr. Hamm. "Superficially, nothing obvious points to cause of death."

Silver-haired and handsome, with twinkling blue-green eyes, Dr. Hamm easily charmed the living, but relished the chance to dally with the dead during a murder investigation.

"No gun or knife wounds?" asked Peter. "Anything under the fingernails? Any bruising?"

"No wounds. No noticeable bruising, but if the bodies froze soon after an assault, the bruising process would be disrupted. Similarly, we would expect to see livor mortis in the legs and buttocks if the victims died in the position they were found."

"Livor mortis as in the blood settling to the lowest parts of the body after death."

"Exactly. In this case, no livor mortis means blood and body fluids would have frozen before they had a chance to settle."

Peter mused that, for a small-town sheriff, he was becoming well-versed in murder. "But, no autopsy until the bodies are thawed?"

"Sorry, no. Just like a turkey, thawing can't be rushed."

"I understand. Thanks, Doc." Peter set down the phone receiver and leaned back in his chair to think. Startled, he almost fell over in his chair when the phone rang. *I've got to stop doing that,* he thought as he picked up the receiver to answer. "Sheriff Elliott."

"Hey, Peter, it's Paul. We need to talk."

Two years older than Peter but slighter in build, with darker hair and a scholarly air, Paul generally wandered through life emitting an aura of peace and calm despite the drama and conflict that came with being the pastor of a small town church. Today, an unusual hint of worry filled his voice.

"Sure," said Peter. "What's going on?"

"No . . . we need to talk in person."

"Is everything okay?"

"Um . . . I hope so. Can you come to the church?"

"I'll be right there." Peter dropped the receiver and grabbed his coat and hat. He whistled to Zack as he hurried through the outer office. "I'll be out for a while, Travis," he said as he ran past.

"Everything okay, Boss?" asked Travis to Peter's disappearing back.

PETER'S PARENTS HAD been robbed and murdered during an anniversary celebration in the city of Missoula when the boys were children. After the murder, Peter and Paul were taken from their home in nearby Princeton and moved to Anderson where they were raised by elderly grandparents.

While eight-year-old Peter felt anger and the need for justice, reflective ten-year-old Paul questioned why. What would cause someone to take another person's life? He studied the people around him and, even at his young age, sensed a hurting humanity. He realized that hurting people hurt people. If he could help the hurting, he could stop the hurt. His contemplations led him to the church and the church led him to ministry.

Any hint of disruption in his older brother's calm exterior raised alarm bells in Peter. Pulling into the church parking lot, Peter found Paul standing in front of the door, hands folded, deep in prayer. Peter shut off the motor, let Zack out of his kennel compartment, and approached his shivering brother.

"Paul? Are you okay?"

Paul lifted his head. Teardrops, frozen midstream, covered his face. Frost coated his eyelashes and the tips of his hair. He pointed to a white paper nailed to the church door, printed with an anger so intense that the pen ripped through the paper in several places.

Peter read, " 'She got what she deserved!!!!' "

"Who got what she deserved? What's this about, Paul?"

"It's all my fault. I should have called you when it started. I thought we could work it out within the church."

Peter went to his vehicle and retrieved a pair of nitrile gloves and an evidence bag. Back on the stoop, he wiggled the nail out of the door and dropped it with the note into the bag. "Let's go inside," he said. "It's freezing out here."

Paul followed Peter into the church and through the chapel. Small, but adequate for the population, the room was a step back in time. Wooden pews polished to a high shine stood in even rows separated by a central aisle. Single arched stained glass windows depicting scenes from the life and death of Jesus Christ allowed sunlight to bathe each pew with a warm glow. In concession to worldly comforts, the pews were padded and upholstered in a sturdy, but bright cardinal red tweed.

Beyond the chapel, a short hallway led to Paul's study. He flipped a switch to start the kettle heating and moved the lever on the wall thermostat to warm the room.

When they were settled into chairs, Peter asked, "Do you want to start at the beginning?"

"No better place," said Paul. "Alice Celares is who the note is referring to. I believe I mentioned she and Frank are part of my congregation."

"You did, when we were notifying Tony of the murders."

"Alice has been the church secretary/treasurer for . . . well, decades. Longer than I've been the pastor." He glanced at Peter. "I trust her completely. There's never been a hint of impropriety."

"But something happened?"

Paul took a deep breath. He stood, walked to the now hot teapot, and poured a cup each for himself and Peter. Handing tea to Peter and settling back into his own chair, he continued, "You know how we have special offerings for things . . . raising money for new carpeting, missionary support, sending the kids to summer camp . . ."

Peter nodded. He regularly donated to those causes.

"Well, a few weeks ago we took a collection to pay for headstones for those kids who were killed in the bus accident. Two of them only have metal stakes for grave markers."

"Are those boys' families members of the church?"

"Not the ones without the markers. Bill and Kathy Edwards, you know, Tom's brother and his wife. Their son Jason was one of the boys killed. He has a nice grave marker. The other boys, well . . . Asher's mom is struggling to pay funeral costs and Carl's mom and her boyfriend don't seem to care. I think the Roost took up a collection for the burial. As far as I know, there wasn't a funeral."

"So, Bill and Kathy requested a special collection for the other boys?"

"Along with Frank and Alice. Frank wasn't legally liable for the accident, but he still felt guilty . . . if he had taken the curve a little slower or handled the slide better . . ." Paul sipped his tea. "Frank knew if he and Alice tried to pay for the stones themselves, the offer would be rejected."

"Why is that?"

"If the person who murdered our parents tried to give you a check for their funeral, would you take it?"

Peter thought for a moment. "No amount of money would bring our parents back. It would be an insult."

"Exactly. Frank wanted to help. The only way was anonymously through the church. Frank and Alice are good friends with Bill and Kathy. The four of them came to me and asked for my guidance. I suggested a special collection."

"They were friends even after the accident? No hard feelings?"

"Not that I could see. If anything, they became closer."

Peter waited, guessing what was coming, but let Paul tell the story.

Paul sighed. "After the collection, the money went missing." He shook his head. "I don't understand it. Who would take money from those kids? Those families?"

"Take me through the collection process," said Peter. "At what point did the money go missing?"

"We have two wooden collection boxes on the back table for church goers to deposit tithing as they come into the sanctuary. One is a replica of the church building. They know that one is for regular tithing. The other one is a plain square box, but 'special' is engraved on the lid so people know it's for special collections."

"How easy would it be for someone to come in and take the money?"

"Almost impossible. The boxes are locked. Only members designated to count and document the collection, usually from the women's bible study, have a key. Besides me, of course."

"Couldn't someone take the boxes?"

With a sheepish look, Paul explained, "A few years ago, someone did come in and steal the boxes. We figured it was during prayer time when we all had our eyes closed and heads bowed. After that, we bolted the boxes to the table."

"So, when did your special collection go missing?"

"When the ladies were done counting, they put the money in a bank bag and then into the safe in my office."

"Are you positive the counters put the money in the safe?"

"Absolutely. They don't have the combination. I had to open it for them."

"So, you saw the bank bag go into the safe. Did you check the bag to verify it had money in it?"

"Uh, no, but the ladies were together when they put the money in the bag and they were together when they brought it to the safe. I've never had a reason to check the bag."

"Until you have two volunteers working a scam together."

"NO! No, no, no. I know these women. They would never do something like that."

Peter, with a strong faith in the corruption of mankind, sighed. "Okay. When did you notice the money missing?"

"Alice came a few days later so she could make the deposit."

"Did you open the safe for her?"

"No. She has the combination."

"She opened the safe and the bag was empty?"

"That's what she said."

"Was she alone when this happened?"

"Yes."

"And you stand by your conviction that she wouldn't steal the money?"

"Absolutely. All the years she's been making the bank deposits, there's never been so much as a cent missing."

"So, sometime between the money going into the bag and Alice taking the bag out of the safe, the money went missing."

"It sounds unlikely, but, yes."

"Who else knows the combination to the safe?"

"Only Alice and me . . . oh, and Linda."

Linda, Paul's wife and head of the Baptist women's group, was not on Peter's list of corrupted mankind. He would need to have a neutral party consider her involvement.

Peter glanced around the office. "Where is this safe?"

Paul smiled, stood, and grabbed the edge of a framed depiction of the crucifixion hanging on the wall behind his desk. The picture swung to the side, revealing a hidden wall safe. "Corny, I know, but nobody has ever figured out it was here."

"That you know of," said Peter, standing to inspect the safe. "No sign of forced entry."

"Nope."

"Who else has been in here? Anyone from outside the church? Cleaners? Contractors?"

"Not in several months."

"And there's never been money missing in the past?"

"Not a cent. In fact, the final deposits are usually for more than what's counted from the collection box."

"How does that work?"

"Alice adds her and Frank's tithe before she deposits. The point is, there is . . . was, never less."

Remembering why he was there, Peter said, "Any idea who would leave that note on the door and why?"

"Obviously someone who believes Alice stole the money."

"No other controversies going on in the church?"

"Nothing significant. People are always arguing about which worship songs should be on the program and whose turn it is to bring cookies. So far snickerdoodles haven't led to murder."

Peter contemplated the daunting task of interviewing everyone in the church. In his favor, as with many rural communities, churches in Anderson were as plentiful as the population was scanty, leaving each pastor with a manageable congregation.

"Can you give me a list of church members?" he asked.

Paul hesitated. "I don't want to imagine one of my congregants stooping to robbery."

"Any more than I want to imagine one of my deputies stooping to murder," said Peter, thinking about Tom. "But, people are people and none of us are immune from temptation."

"You're preaching to the preacher, little brother," Paul grinned. "Maybe you missed your calling."

"Nope. You preach the gospel and I'll lock up the bad guys. If you could, put a star by the names of the ladies who counted the collection money."

Paul rubbed his temples, easing the tension of a headache. He opened his top desk drawer and took out a copy of the church directory. He starred two names and slid the booklet across his desk to Peter.

10

Exhausted from a day of interviews, Angus drug himself up the courthouse stairs to the second floor. Close at his heels, he heard the click, click of Zack's claws as Peter and Zack made their way to the sheriff's office. Inside, they found Helen and Travis bent over the work table, studying piles of documents.

"Find anything interesting?" asked Peter to their bent heads.

Helen glanced in his direction. "Maybe. What did Alice Celares do for a living?"

Peter shrugged and looked at Angus. "Any idea?"

"No. Why?"

"Well," said Helen, "for a bus driver and a housewife, which I'm guessing because I can't find any source of income for her, they did well for themselves."

"How so?" asked Peter, pulling a chair up to the table.

Helen showed him bank statements and an investment portfolio.

"Okay," he said. "Decent, but nothing that raises red flags."

"Look at this." Helen showed him a file of Frank's pay stubs. "How does that income add up to these investments and savings?"

"We can't jump to conclusions," said Peter. "Maybe they lived on an inheritance."

"I always wondered," said Helen, "how Tony could afford that fancy college back east. He was a mediocre student and, other than bowling, wasn't an athlete. Nothing that would have gotten him a full-ride scholarship."

"Number one rule . . ." said Peter.

"I know, I know. Don't assume."

"Anything else?"

"Nothing. No debts. Everything in order. Whether it was Frank or Alice keeping records, they were very well organized."

"Speaking of money," said Peter. He told the story of Alice and the missing church collection.

"That could explain the Caleres' healthy bank account," said Helen.

"Paul insisted that, until now, there's never been so much as a penny missing."

He took the evidence bag containing the note and nail out of his duty vest and laid it on the table. "Paul found this nailed to the church door this morning."

"Who got what she deserved?" asked Angus.

"Paul thinks the note refers to Alice Celares . . . because of the missing money."

"Who left the note then?" asked Travis. "The murderer?"

"Or someone giving the murderer a thumbs-up." Peter handed the bag to Travis. "Add this to your list for fingerprints."

"On it, Boss."

Peter glanced at Angus. "How did your interviews go?"

Angus told them about his visit with Angela Brown. "She definitely blames Frank for her son's death and she lied about having visitors or leaving the property herself. Tire tracks going into her place would have happened after the snow."

"Any chance of matching the tracks to her vehicle?"

Angus grinned. "She drives a beat-up old farm truck. I parked right next to her, and took pictures of the tires on my side when I left. No way she would have seen me. There's a thick grove of aspen at the turnoff to her lane blocking her vision of the road. The tire tracks were spread out enough to get clear pictures."

Angus took out his camera and passed the comparison pictures around for everyone to study.

"Sure looks like the same tires," said Travis.

"Enough to warrant a stakeout," agreed Peter. "Are you up for overtime, Angus?"

"Sure. That aspen grove is a perfect place to park." Angus then said, "Oh, yeah," pulling the broken cup handle out of his pocket, he told them about Angela dropping her coffee cup. "This should have her fingerprints if we ever need them."

Angus took an evidence bag out of his duty vest and dropped in the handle, careful only to touch it on the broken edges.

Travis took the bag. "I'll give this to Clem."

That settled, Peter asked, "What did you find out about the other parents?"

"The second boy was Carl Revell. I found June Revell and her boyfriend down at the Roost and got the typical response, 'We know nothing. We saw nothing'."

"Any thoughts on them as suspects?"

"Way down on the list," he told them about his chat with Vern Davis. "From what Vern told me, they kicked the kid out years ago."

"Paul was under the impression that the Roost took up a collection for Carl's burial, but there wasn't a funeral," said Peter. "I agree. That mom isn't shedding any tears. How about the third boy?"

"Jason Edwards. Parents are Bill and Kathy Edwards," said Angus. He glanced at the others. "Tom's brother and his wife. They weren't home. I called Tom and he said they're out of town visiting relatives for Christmas."

"Do you think Tom tipped them off?" asked Travis, a blush creeping up his face, embarrassed at questioning the motives of an Anderson deputy.

"According to Paul," said Peter, "Bill and Kathy were close friends of Frank and Alice before the accident and became closer afterwards. There's no indication they would be suspects of a revenge killing for the accident or the missing church funds. Regardless, we can't give them a pass. Angus, see if you can track them down."

"Got it."

"So, we've narrowed down Angela Brown as the main suspect for the bus accident motive and gained a church full of suspects for the missing money motive," said Peter. He glanced at his watch as Helen walked through the door, ready to clock out from her shift. Quitting time. "Anything else?"

Everyone shook their heads 'no.'

"Okay, we'll start up again tomorrow," said Peter. Not for the first time, he studied his crew, aware that they were all single and going home to empty houses. A symptom of the shallow dating pool in a small town, the stresses of a law enforcement career, or both? Travis, infatuated with Birdie, had yet to make that connection stick. Angus shamelessly chased an oblivious Holly Noelle, Peter's ex-girlfriend and owner of The Sapphire Pit gem mine. Peter considered Helen. Deserted and divorced from her cheating ex-husband, hair slipping back into the long gray braid of earlier years and weight climbing. What happened to her blooming romance with Adam Henry, the police academy instructor from Helena? Peter sighed and whistled to Zack, thinking of his own empty bungalow. His thoughts paused on his childhood friend turned woman, Dixie, with the pixie face and cornflower blue eyes. He needed to call her.

⚬⚬⚬❖⚬⚬⚬

LIMPING HOME TO his own abode, expecting a chilly welcome from his wife, Tony Celares contemplated the empty space left in his life with the death of his parents and vowed to fix his marriage. Maybe a surprise trip to somewhere warm would thaw Susan's icy heart. He opened the door and called, "Susan! I'm home!" as something heavy landed a solid blow on the back of his head.

11

BLINDFOLDED AND GAGGED, wrists and ankles bound, head pounding, Tony Celares fought nausea and panic. Thin, coarse carpeting scraped the skin on his face as jarring movements tossed him against the sides of his prison. Sounds of the road and the odor of gasoline brought him to the realization that he was trapped in a car en route to an unknown location. How long he had been traveling, he didn't know, but the journey ended soon after he became aware. He listened as the driver stopped the vehicle and exited the car. Next came the rattling of a garage door opening. The driver returned, drove into the garage, and switched off the engine. The garage door rattled to the floor and metal clanged as locks slid into place.

Hearing the hatchback door of the car open next to him, Tony struggled against his bindings.

"You're wasting your time," said a voice.

A familiar voice. Tony struggled to clear his mind of panic and place the voice with a person.

Hands grasped his thick down coat at the shoulders and pulled him roughly from the car. They dragged him a short distance and dropped him onto what felt like padded concrete. Pain took precedence over fear. The jarring added pain to his already pounding head and gouty toe.

"What do you want," he said through the gag, no matter that it came out as unintelligible gibber. His pleas went unheard behind the closing of a door.

In the following silence, Tony willed himself to be calm, to think. He struggled to recall his last memories before he woke up in the car. Coming home, calling out to Susan.

Susan! Where's Susan?

12

DECLARED AN OFFICIAL town holiday decades past, the *Day of Lights* outshone even murder in the minds of most residents of Anderson. Floats must be built, lights strung, and bags of candy and goodies filled for expectant spectators. Regardless of the required preparations, Peter's responsibility remained with the investigation.

The following day he walked into a near deserted office, phones forwarded, and deputies busy with holiday festivities. Waiting patiently in the outer office, Clementine Smith sat dressed for a western parade in a royal blue split skirt, matching riding jacket, and a gunmetal gray wool hat trailing a wide silk ribbon.

"Dressed for the occasion, I see," said Peter.

Clem sighed. "Longest day of the year in Anderson. Starts at dawn and ends after dark."

"Please tell me you're not planning to lasso me into judging the chili contest."

Clem laughed. "All judges accounted for. All you have to do is show up for the parade and keep Archie pointed in the right direction."

"Good. Last year I had heartburn for a week." Motioning her into his office, Peter said, "Cup of tea? I can boil it in the microwave so we don't have to wait for the electric pot."

"Sounds perfect. Thank you." She settled into a comfortable leather chair in front of Peter's desk and thanked him again when he handed her a cup.

"So, what's up?" he asked.

"A couple of things. First, I've processed the prints from the murder house. I need comparison prints from the deceased . . . and anyone else who may have been in the house legitimately. The prints from the church door note were mostly smeared, but there were partials. At this time of year, everyone is wearing gloves, so no surprise there."

"I'll stop by the morgue and collect prints from the bodies and ask Tony who else would have been there. Anything else?"

Clem cleared her throat. "That file you gave me a few months ago . . . the one on your parents' murder—"

"Yeah?"

"I've begun an investigation, starting with the restaurant where they ate dinner that night. As you would imagine, over twenty years later, most of the workers are long gone."

"Most?"

"As it happens, the current manager was a young busboy at the time, and remembers the murder well."

Peter sat up straight and braced himself on his desk. "He remembers?" He swallowed, feeling mildly nauseous. "Does he know anything about what happened?"

"He wants to talk in person. I'm heading over there this week. I thought you should know."

Stunned speechless, Peter's heart raced and he rubbed his face as he tried to collect himself.

"Are you going to be okay?" asked Clem.

"Yeah, it's just, after all these years—"

Clem stood and straightened her jacket. "I'll keep you posted. See you at the parade."

Memories of his parents flooded Peter's mind until a loud boom and extended crackling startled him out of his revery. Fireworks. Three times during the year fireworks were allowed within city limits: Independence Day, New Year's, and Day of Lights. The town would be popping and crackling until the wee hours of the morning.

Zack, tolerant of the noise, but not a fan, preferred to stay close to Peter during these times. Peter took a bully stick out of a stash in his bottom drawer and flipped it to Zack. "No donuts today, but this'll keep your mind off the noise."

In an effort to keep his own mind on the current murder, Peter grabbed his hat and coat off the hook behind his desk and whistled to Zack. "Come on, Zack. We need to visit the morgue."

IN THE ALLEY behind the hospital, a cement ramp led the way to a set of double doors opening into the basement morgue. Rather than going through the hospital and the process of explaining himself to curious front desk attendants, Peter parked in the alley, left the heater running for Zack, and knocked on the double doors. A young morgue attendant lifted the curtain on a side window, recognized Peter, and let him in.

"Howdy, Sheriff. What's up?"

"I need fingerprints from the Celareses."

"For the *crime scene investigation*. Cool!" He led Peter to a bank of corpse refrigerators and pulled out two middle drawers where Frank and Alice lay side by side, still mostly frozen.

Peter laid out a fingerprinting kit on a side table and quickly filled fingerprint cards. He thanked the attendant and headed back to his vehicle.

As he settled into his seat, his phone binged. Tom. "Hey, Tom. What's up?"

"Where are you?"

"Just leaving the morgue. Why?"

"You need to come to the grocery store! Fast! And bring backup!"

"What?! What's going on?" asked Peter as he shifted into gear and roared out of the alley.

"Mavis and the mayor. They've started a riot."

"I'm on my way." He toggled the button on his radio and spoke to Travis, "I need backup at the grocery store. Anyone available."

13

A BLUE AND WHITE van from KRUD TV out of Missoula sat in the middle of the grocery store parking lot. Alongside the television crew and cameras, Mavis Vallee, editor-in-chief and sole reporter of the local weekly, *The Anderson Chronicle*, stood primping and preening, waiting for her turn in the spotlight. Rarely seen wearing anything less than a well-cut pantsuit, towering high heels, and perfectly coifed platinum hair, Mavis was ever ready for a coveted television appearance even if that meant manufacturing a drama and calling the television station herself.

Mayor Dwight Kalinski, mayor only because the previous mayor and more popular candidate died of a heart attack on election night, strutted across an insta-stage, bellowing into a microphone, seemingly unaware of the brawl taking place in the parking lot below.

"Sheriff Elliott is a disgrace! A disgrace I say, not only to the town of Anderson, but to the entirety of Stone County! We must stand up to his supporters and fight for justice."

Peter pulled into the parking lot and surveyed a scene of chaos. Men bloodied and bruised, trading punches; a woman pummeling another with a loaf of French bread; children clenched in wrestling holds. Shopping carts over-turned, canned foods and various fruits rolling freely across the lot, dozens of broken eggs. Peter noticed wryly that many of the broken eggs had managed to jump out of their cartons and throw themselves at people and cars. Across the lot, a group of teenage boys attempted to lob a large rock into the plate glass front of the store. Switching on his siren and using his bullhorn, Peter demanded, "Sit where you are and put your hands on your heads. You are all on dash cam so don't even think of leaving or you'll be charged with resisting arrest."

The boys turned, dazed, and dropped the rock, which landed square on the foot of one of the hooligans who, likewise, jumped up and down, screeching in pain. All other action stopped, faces turned toward Peter, most with wide-eyed expressions of guilt and dismay.

Helen's patrol vehicle slid into the other side of the lot, blocking the exit. Angus pulled up to the middle curb. Each flipped on their lights and jumped out of their vehicles.

Mayor Kalinski, smugly sure of himself and basking in the glow of the television lights, continued his rant while the television cameras frantically filmed in every direction. Mavis grabbed a microphone and hopped onto the stage, determined to have her own spot in the limelight before Peter shut things down.

Out of his vehicle, Peter released Zack from his kennel compartment, pulled the handcuffs from his duty belt, and ran to the stage.

He motioned Angus toward the crowd in front of the store. "Don't let anyone leave."

He turned toward Helen. "Arrest Mavis."

"Inciting a riot," he said to Helen's questioning look.

Peter jumped onto the stage and headed for the mayor. Taking the microphone and dropping it onto the stage, he pulled the mayor's hands behind his back and slapped on the cuffs.

"What do you think you're doing?!" bellowed Kalinski.

"You're under arrest for inciting a riot."

Helen, not inclined to jump, found a set of stairs leaning against the side stage. She climbed up and cuffed a now stunned Mavis. Mavis, shocked into silence, allowed Helen to lead her off the stage and into Helen's waiting patrol vehicle.

Mayor Kalinski blustered and howled and threatened the entire way. "You'll all be fired! I'll have you in jail before the day's out!" Pulling back from being put into the rear of Peter's patrol vehicle, the mayor relented with a warning growl from Zack.

With Mavis and the mayor safely stowed, Peter, Helen, and Angus returned to deal with the rest of the crowd, most of them coming down off the high of mob mentality and in stark realization of their predicament.

Peter pulled his phone out of his duty belt and punched in a number. He breathed a sigh of relief when Tom answered.

"Everything okay in there?" Peter asked.

"Yeah, we're a little shook up. We locked the door and barricaded ourselves in the office when things got squirrely."

"Give us a bit to get this crowd taken care of and you should be safe to come out."

"Got it. Thanks, Peter."

Peter disconnected and surveyed the disheveled crowd. Splintered remains of what Peter realized were picket signs lay scattered here and there amongst bruised bananas and soggy paper cartons. He walked over and read the hand-lettered message on a sign leaning against a well-egged car with Missoula County license plates. *Tom Edwards is a Murderer!* Another sign lying on the ground nearby stated *Sheriff Elliott Protects Murderers!* Peter clenched his teeth and willed himself to control his anger.

Retrieving his bullhorn from his vehicle, he faced the crowd and bellowed, "If any of you have injuries that require medical care, please notify myself or one of the deputies." He looked pointedly at the teenager with the rock injured foot who shook his head and gave Peter a thumbs-up.

While Helen and Angus walked the crowd for injuries, one man raised his hand.

"Do you have an injury?" asked Helen.

"No . . . it's just, my wife had nothing to do with this. She's been sitting in the car with the kids the whole time. Can she go home?"

"Where's your vehicle?"

He pointed to a dirty gray Chevy Tahoe. Helen walked over to the passenger side window where a sullen-faced woman bounced a crying baby on her knee. Two older children sat strapped in car seats in the rear. The woman lowered the window at Helen's request.

"Ma'am, your husband tells me you weren't involved in the incident."

"I told him to stay out of it and mind his own business! I shoulda' left him here."

"Okay, ma'am. As soon as we clear the parking lot, you're free to go, but for everyone's safety, please wait until we give you the go-ahead."

Helen walked over and explained the situation to Peter and Angus, who had finished his canvas of the injured.

"Okay," said Peter. "Since nobody's admitting to a serious injury, check the rest of the vehicles for folks who weren't involved."

He raised the bullhorn and announced, "All of you will be taken to jail and charged with disorderly conduct. Since the sheriff's department doesn't own a bus, you will be walking to the courthouse. After processing, you will be given the chance to pay bail and will be free to go."

The announcement was met with groans and grumbling as he continued, "Everyone stand and form a line starting here." He pointed to a spot in front of where he was standing.

Angus helped organize the line of twenty-seven men, women, and children.

Helen found several cars whose drivers had pulled into the parking lot or had been ready to leave with their groceries when the riot began. As possible witnesses, their names and addresses were taken down and they were instructed to wait until the parking lot was cleared of people before leaving.

"We could use an extra person," Helen commented to Peter as she studied the line. "Are we going to make Mavis and the mayor walk, too?"

"We should, but no. I'll walk with this group. Take Mavis, book her, and put her in my office."

Helen left and Peter pulled Angus aside. "Listen, there could be questions of conflict of interest so I need to step back. Take my vehicle with the mayor. You'll be in charge of questioning him and Mavis. We need proof for the inciting a riot charge to stick so focus on that."

"Got it," said Angus as he turned and made his way to Peter's vehicle. He steeled himself for an unpleasant trip to the courthouse. Surprised by a quiet reception, Angus started the vehicle and prepared to drive away when the indignant mayor resumed his tirade.

"What?! Where are we going?! I demand you release me."

Angus pushed the button on his police radio. "Travis, prepare a cell."

14

WATCHING WITH RELIEF as Angus, rather than Peter, walked into Peter's office, Mavis put on what she thought was her most charming smile.

"Oh, Angus, I'm so sorry for this misunderstanding," she crooned. "Peter does have a temper, doesn't he?"

Her smile faded when she saw the cold blue steel in Angus's eyes. Angus flipped through the file cabinet, took out a Waiver of Rights form and settled into the comfortable leather chair behind Peter's desk.

"Mavis Vallee, you are being charged with inciting a riot," said Angus. "Do you understand the charges against you?"

"Whatever do you mean, Angus? That little disagreement in the parking lot was hardly a riot."

Opening a handbook of Montana criminal law statutes, Angus flipped through until he came to the definition of riot and read a condensed version.

"A person commits the offense of riot if the person purposely and knowingly disturbs the peace by engaging in an act of violence as part of an assemblage of five or more persons and the act results in damage of property or injury to persons." He looked pointedly at Mavis. "There were more than five people involved in that 'little disagreement' and there were definitely injuries to persons and damage to property. Egged cars. Litter scattered across the parking lot."

"Well, okay," said Mavis. "Technically, that could be considered a riot, but what does it have to do with me?"

Angus looked down at the book. "A person commits the offense of incitement to riot if the person purposely and knowingly commits an act or engages in conduct that urges other persons to riot." He studied Mavis's puzzled face as he asked again, "Do you understand these charges?"

"Well, I guess so, Angus, but I still don't understand what they have to do with me."

Angus recited the Miranda warning. "Would you like a lawyer before we continue questioning?"

"I've done nothing wrong, Angus. And, frankly, I'm offended at the suggestion." She signed the waiver form Angus slid across the desk and crossed her arms against her chest, giving him a defiant look.

"Mavis, please explain to me how KRUD TV out of Missoula happened to be in the grocery store parking lot today."

"I . . . uh . . . that is the mayor and I . . . uh, we thought it prudent, well, that the public had a right to know . . ." She swallowed hard.

"The public had a right to know what?"

"Well, that a suspect in a vicious murder was running free in the community."

"You're referring to Tom Edwards."

"Yes, of course."

"Mavis, what evidence do you have that Tom had anything to do with those murders?"

"Well . . . uh, no actual evidence, I guess."

"Exactly. Neither do we. That's why Tom hasn't been arrested."

Mavis attempted another smile. "You know, Angus, with Peter out of the way, you're a shoo-in for the next election."

Clenching his teeth and slowly counting to ten, Angus controlled his temper. "Ms. Vallee, did you or the mayor make the call to the television station?"

"Well, I did, Angus, but only after the mayor and I discussed the situation. It was all for the good of the community."

"Sure. Did you mention specific names during that call?"

"Well . . . I may have mentioned that Tom Edwards owns the grocery store—"

"Did you mention the sheriff in your conversation?"

"Oh . . . he may have come up."

"Yes or no, did you mention the sheriff?"

"Yes," said Mavis angrily, "I mentioned the sheriff putting our citizens at risk by letting a murder suspect run free. Does this department not recognize our constitutional rights of freedom of speech? Does freedom of the press not mean anything to you?!"

"Sure they do. You have the right to tell nasty lies about anybody you choose. What you don't have a right to is inciting or participating in a riot. You also don't have a right to special treatment. Everyone in that parking lot who participated in that riot was arrested, including you and the mayor."

Mavis pressed her lips together, crossed her arms, and huffed.

"I noticed picket signs leaning against cars with Missoula County plates," said Angus. "Can you explain that?"

"We do have a lovely grocery store," said Mavis with a smile, in a desperate attempt to turn the conversation in her favor. "I imagine visitors enjoy driving down to do their shopping."

"In the middle of winter? From Missoula? With picket signs?"

"Oh, all right. The mayor mentioned having a few friends in Missoula who would be willing to picket for a fee. I didn't have anything to do with that!"

Slapping his notebook shut, Angus left the room, ignoring Mavis's pleas for release and made his way to the jail cells downstairs.

The mayor's attitude had not improved. Quiet and contemplative in his cell alone, as soon as he saw Angus, he began spewing venom and threats. Patience depleted, Angus stepped out, closed the door, and went upstairs to the sheriff's office where Peter was writing tickets and Zack worked the crowd for belly rubs and ear scratches.

"Mavis admitted to calling KRUD," said Angus, pulling Peter aside. "She says it was the mayor who arranged the picketers."

"What does the mayor say?"

"Nothing repeatable in polite company. I think he needs a few more hours in his cell to cool down."

"Did he lawyer up?"

"He threatens, but so far, no."

"Okay, let him sit. When he realizes threats are getting him nowhere, he might change his tune."

Angus stifled a grin. "What about Mavis?"

"Is she behaving herself?"

"Pretty much."

"An investigation may clear her but write the ticket for now. If she pays bail, let her go. Oh, and I separated the picketers from the local group. They're in cells downstairs. See if you can get anything out of them."

"Got it."

Angus went into Peter's office where Mavis waited impatiently. After she agreed to pay bail, he looked her in the eye, and said, "Peter made the decision to release you. You should thank him before you leave," he paused. "And an apology wouldn't hurt."

RELAXING AT THE worktable after the last brawler left clutching a bail receipt, Peter smelled the distinctive odor of pizza wafting down the hallway leading to the sheriff's office. His stomach growled. "Did someone order pizza?"

"Right on time," said Angus with a grin as Bud Henderson, owner of the Moonlight Mountain Brewery, walked in carrying a pizza box.

"Everything, but the kitchen sink. Your favorite," said Bud, setting the box on Travis's desk.

Peter thanked Bud, pulled up a chair, and opened the box. Choosing a slice, he took a bite before breaking off a piece for Zack. "Anything new with the mayor?" he asked.

Angus laughed. "You were right. When he realized he wasn't going anywhere, he bent over backwards to apologize."

"Did you get anything out of him?"

"He verified that he paid the protestors and told them what to write on the signs. He was pretty smug about the whole thing, let me know he was on the right side of the law. In the end, he called his lawyer and made bail. Sitting in jail overnight for the cause wasn't worth it to him."

"Do we have a tape of his speech? He was encouraging a fight."

"KRUD TV does. It made the news."

"Oh boy. Did you get anything out of the picketers?"

"When they were talking among themselves, I heard one comment that the mayor told them to 'get a fight started,' but they lawyered up when I tried to question them. In the end, everyone paid bail and went home."

"Good. We have enough going on tonight without worrying about a full jail." Peter finished his pizza and grabbed another slice. "Anything else I need to know about? How'd your stakeout go, Angus?"

"A bust. She fed her animals and went inside. Lights out around ten. I left."

"We'll catch her another night. Everything else quiet in town?"

"As quiet as Day of Lights can be. We've had a few fireworks complaints. Nothing more than singed fingers so far," said Travis. "Oh, yeah, Nancy May called to remind you about the parade in case you forgot."

Peter rolled his eyes and glanced at his watch. "Time to get into costume."

15

STARTLED OUT OF an exhausted sleep, Tony felt hands pulling at the gag around his mouth. As it loosened and dropped to his chin, the familiar voice of his abductor asked, "Where's the loot?"

"What loot? What are you talking about?" rasped Tony, mouth dry from the gag. "Where's my wife? Where's Susan?"

A heavy boot kicked at Tony's ribs.

"Where's the loot?" asked the voice again.

"Look, I don't know about any loot." He needed time to think.

What loot?

"Listen, I need to use the bathroom. Could we do that first?"

A moment passed.

"No funny business," said the voice. "Nothing to stop me putting a bullet through your head."

Tony heard a snap and felt the zip tie binding his wrists release. "Get up!"

Blocking out the burn in his toe and pounding in his head, Tony struggled to his feet. His abductor led him across the garage and through a doorway to a room with a familiar scent. Whoever lived here used the same air freshener as Susan. *Susan.*

"Where's Susan? Where's my wife?"

The hand holding Tony's arm led him to a spot. He felt cold porcelain through his pants.

"Can you remove the blindfold? So I can see what I'm doing?"

More laughter. "You're facing the right direction. What do I care if you miss? I don't have to clean."

Tony did his business as best he could and refastened his pants. Reaching up, he touched the back of his head and winced with pain. Blood from the wound matted his hair and trickled down the back of his neck.

"Hands together. Tight," said the voice.

Tony did as he was told and felt new zip ties fasten around his wrists. His abductor led him back across the garage.

"On the floor!" ordered the voice.

Tony lowered himself onto the mat.

"Where's the loot?"

With one discomfort eliminated and a need to buy more time, Tony said, "My head's pounding. I can hardly think. Do you have any pain medicine?"

A pause. "What kind of pain medicine?" asked the voice.

"Anything. Don't you take something for a headache?"

"Yeah, well, I'll look around."

While his captor did his bidding, Tony wracked his brain. *Loot? What loot? Is this why my parents were murdered?*

A cold glass bumped against his face. "Here's your pills. Open your mouth."

Four tablets dropped into Tony's mouth and cold water poured onto his face. He caught enough in his mouth to swallow the pills without choking. The medicine would take time to work its magic, but relief was on the way. He considered his situation. His captor was not coming across as a hardened criminal, but judging by his parents' fate, capable of murder. Fear, pain, and the thump on his head kept Tony's brain muddled.

Something heavy slammed against the wall, making Tony jump. "Last time," said the voice. "The loot! Where is it? Now!!!"

"I . . . I . . . don't know what you're talking about. What loot?"

A barrage of heavy thuds against the wall made Tony cringe. He thought of the destruction in his parents' house and the way they died. Aware of the rumble of an over-head heater and the soothing warmth it brought, Tony wondered how long he had before that heat was turned off and he was left to freeze to death like his parents did. *Where's Susan?*

16

N IGHT FALLS EARLY during the winter months, even more so in the mountains and it was well past dark when Peter arrived at the light parade staging area. In spite of the night, the lot glowed with the warmth of thousands of twinkling lights. Every imaginable entry meandered across the lot—from dogs sporting glow-stick collars to tractors wrapped in tinsel and blinking Christmas lights.

Entries gathered in a wide-open area at the bottom of the hill, close to the highway. Under threats from Nancy May, the county road crew had the lot well plowed before festivities began. As each entrant arrived, Nancy, decked out in fur and diamonds, checked them off a list. A florescent orange vinyl square with black numbers was zip tied somewhere on each entry vehicle or person.

Peter found Seth Geary, reins in hand, standing at the head of the line staring openmouthed at the next-in-line entry. Archie, for all his calm demeanor, turned his big head occasionally at the rattles and clanks coming from the contraption to his rear.

"Nancy," asked Peter, "what is that?!"

"Oh, good, you're here." She turned and smiled lovingly at the quivering hunk of rust. "It's a Cadillac, silly."

Streaks of faded blue, interspersed with rust, colored the exterior. Dents in the hood, reminiscent of hooves in thick mud, explained the layer of dried cow dung splattered across most of the car. Dried into the dung was an assortment of colored feathers. Peter expected a chicken to fly out the window at any moment.

"Hmmmm," he said. "Where did you find this treasure?"

"A barn sale. Been sitting there for decades and it still runs!"

"Amazing." Noticing the driver's side mirror dangling by wires and a broken headlight, Peter asked, "Do you think it's street legal?"

"That doesn't count in a parade. It'll be fixed up good as new before I drive it for real."

Peter sighed. Sometimes it was better to look the other way. "Are we ready to go then?"

Nancy checked her list. "Everyone showed up except Tony Celares. He was supposed to drive the bank float."

"His parents just died. The parade's probably not on the top of his list."

"That's what the others said, but he didn't even call. Anyway, one of the tellers offered to drive." Nancy took a miniature bullhorn out of her roomy fur pocket and bellowed, "Mount up!"

Ears ringing, Peter lifted his left foot into the stirrup, swung himself over Archie's massive back and into the saddle, avoiding the string of lights draped from ears to tail.

Seth handed him the reins. "I'll be here when you get back," he said.

Peter whistled to Zack and gave Archie a cluck and a squeeze. He moved out into the road and up the hill. After years on light parade duty, the old horse hardly needed guidance. Peter settled into his easy sway. The cold spell had broken into a balmy thirty-two degrees and a million stars twinkled through the deep blue mantle of the night sky. Soft, thick snowflakes drifted through the air.

Deep bass bellows broke into Peter's musings, followed by a familiar voice shouting, "Stop! Stop the parade!"

Peter reined Archie to a halt and turned in his saddle. Stony Clairmont, retired sailor and leader of the recently formed 'Rustic Rangers' boys club, trotted to the front of the parade line, shouting and blowing into a replica Viking ox horn.

"What on earth, Stony," said Peter as Stony stopped next to Archie and leaned over gasping, trying to catch his breath.

"I'm gettin' . . . gasp . . . too old fer this nonsense," said Stony.

"I told you that when you came to me with the boy's club idea," said Peter. "What's the problem?"

"WHAT is the problem?" echoed Nancy May, out of her car and checking her watch. "We're five minutes behind schedule."

"It's the Rustler's Roost," explained Stony. "Now I'm no saint, but they're doin' stuff that's makin' me blush . . . and right in front of those boys."

Peter swung his leg over and slid out of the saddle. He handed the reins to Nancy, who gave him a horrified look. "What am I supposed to do with these?"

"Just stand there. He's not going anywhere."

As Peter followed Stony down the parade line, tinny piano music and raucous singing grew louder until they came to a flatbed trailer pulled by a pick-up truck. Christmas lights blinked along the length of the display, but that's where convention ended. At the head of the group, Rustler's Roost's bartender, Eddie, wearing a frock coat and bow tie, sat banging clumsily at a battered upright piano. Next to him stood Mary, singing off key at the top of her lungs. She wore a blood-red, old west dance hall dress complete with black ankle boots and a red lace shawl. Roost patrons sat in wooden saloon chairs dressed in a mixture of traditional western clothing ranging from canvas dusters to a beaver skin top hat. An empty whiskey bottle rolled off the trailer and onto Peter's foot.

At the end of the trailer, Hobo Joe sat in his customary rags teaching a bawdy ballad to a half dozen giggling preadolescent boys.

"See what I mean?" said Stony. "Their parents will have my hide."

"Joe! What are you doing?" asked Peter.

"Aw, come on, Sheriff. We jus' havin' a bit a' fun. Don' tell me you never sung a dirty ditty or two when you wuz a kid."

Peter hesitated. He couldn't honestly say he hadn't. "That's not the point, Joe. I didn't learn them in a saloon."

"What are we gonna' do, Peter?" asked Stony.

"Well, we could move the boys to another spot. Who's next in line?"

Stony rolled his eyes. "The Catholic Ladies Guild."

"Oh, okay, that's not going to work." Peter thought for a moment. "We could move the Roost bunch. Who's driving this rig anyway?"

He walked around to the driver's window and stopped short in surprise. "Linda?"

"Hey, Peter," she said sheepishly.

"What are you doing driving for the Roost crowd?"

"Well . . . Mary asked me and," she glanced toward the back of the truck, "I figured better me than one of them."

"True, but we've got a problem. Those hooligans are tarnishing the innocence of our Rustic Rangers."

"Why don't you have them sing something else?"

"Like what?"

She shrugged, "Christmas carols?"

Peter walked back to the trailer. "Hey, Eddie!" he hollered during a lull in the singing. "Do you know any Christmas music?"

"Naw, only saloon songs."

The truck door opened and Linda hopped out. "I can play," she said.

"Hey, Eddie," hollered Peter. "Have you been drinking?"

"Not a drop." He made an X motion across his chest. "Cross my heart and all that. This is my truck. I have to drive it home tonight."

"Well, you can drive it now. Linda's trading you places."

Peter watched as Eddie hopped off the trailer and helped Linda over the railing. "Joe," he said. "You're riding in front with Eddie. I don't trust you back here with the boys. You probably know all the dirty versions of the Christmas carols."

"And you've got too much starch in yer britches, Sheriff," grumbled Joe, but he saluted the boys and eased himself to the ground. "Never mind me, Eddie. Time to get on home and feed my dogs."

The deep bass of the ox horn sounded through the night as Stony called his troops to attention, followed by Linda's jolly Christmas tunes. Peter returned to Archie and an exasperated Nancy May.

"Ten minutes," she said, handing him Archie's reins and tapping her watch. "Ten minutes off schedule."

Peter grabbed her, swung her around, and gave her a peck on the cheek, "It'll be fine, Nancy. We'll make up the time on the straight-away."

"Well . . . well . . ."

✦

A PRETTY TOWN during ordinary seasons, Anderson outdid itself at Christmastime. Every shop window held a Christmas scene that every next window tried to outdo, no matter that the contest prize was the honor of a faded purple ribbon passed back and forth from year to year. Wreaths adorned old-fashioned street lamps, lights sparkled on every tree, and groups of carolers stood at street corners, taking turns serenading the parade.

So engrossed was Peter in the spirit of the season, he didn't realize anything was wrong until people on the boardwalk began shouting and pointing behind him. Turning in the saddle, he noticed in astonishment that he was alone in the road. Several blocks down, the front half of the parade formed a ragged line into a side street. The rest milled about in a jumbled knot at the intersection. Peter's heart raced when the alarm for the volunteer fire department began to wail and dogs began to howl. He turned Archie toward the melee, clucking and squeezing in an attempt at a walk rather than a plod.

Avoiding the chaos as he neared the intersection, Peter took to the boardwalk. Hearing the clomp of horse hooves, parade goers backed into doorways to give Archie room. As Peter rounded the corner, he saw flames boiling out of the hood of a rusty blue Cadillac. His heart sank. He slid off Archie and handed the reins to a reliable looking fellow watching from the shadows and ran toward the car, yelling, "Nancy! Nancy!"

The fire department and EMTs were already on site. Having anticipated chaos on Main Street, they drove the back way around.

EMT Scott Haugen called out to Peter as he ran past the ambulance, "Peter! Nancy's over here."

Sitting inside the open rear doors of the ambulance, Nancy held an oxygen mask against her face. When she saw Peter, she lifted the mask away, coughed, and said in a raspy voice, "Oh, Peter, my poor car."

"What happened?" asked Peter, relief catching in his throat.

Nancy took a few more deep breaths from the oxygen mask and sputtered, "Everything was fine and then smoke started coming out of the hood—"

"We need to get her to the hospital," said Scott as Nancy broke into a fit of coughing. He and another attendant helped her onto the gurney and signaled to the ambulance driver they needed to go.

"Is she going to be okay?" asked Peter.

Scott shrugged. "Dr. Hamm is at the hospital waiting for us. She's in good hands."

Fire extinguished and ambulance on its way to the hospital, townsfolk relaxed and the Light Parade morphed into a street party. Peter collected Archie who was busy chomping sliced apples someone had conjured from the steak house down the street. Peter mounted and turned Archie toward the staging area. As much as Nancy was a beloved part of the community, as far as Peter knew, she had no family. He wasn't going to let her be alone in the hospital.

"Thanks, Seth," he said as he handed over Archie's reins and gave him a final scratch under the chin. "See you next year, Archie."

"You could come to visit now and then," said Seth. "Maybe even take him out for a ride."

Peter nodded. "I might do that." He ran to his vehicle and took the side streets to his bungalow where he dropped off Zack. "Sorry, Zack, the hospital frowns on dogs in the ER." He then made his way to the hospital and parked by the rear emergency room entrance.

Somber looks on the faces of the nurses made his heart sink. Dr. Hamm came out of a curtained room and pulled him aside.

"She's stable now, but we'll keep her here overnight under observation. If she hadn't got out of that car when she did, we would have lost her. Smoke inhalation is serious for everyone but especially deadly for older folks."

"Can I see her?"

Dr. Hamm patted his arm. "Let her sleep." He pointed toward the waiting area. "We'll keep you updated."

17

PETER WOKE THE next morning stiff and uncomfortable on a waiting room couch. During the night, someone had covered him in a white hospital blanket, but the hard plastic arm rest dug into his cheek. He sat up, yawned loudly, and stretched.

"Good morning sleepy head," said the nurse manning the desk.

Peter nodded toward the curtain pulled across the doorway to Nancy's room. "How's she doing?"

"Full of piss and vinegar. Go on in and find out."

"I heard that!" yelled a hoarse voice behind the curtain.

Peter laughed. "She's back."

NANCY RELEASED AND home safe, Peter contemplated his day. Two murders needed solving, the victims possibly targets for different motives. Through Angus's questioning they had a bead on the bus accident parents, but the church angle was hanging in the wind.

Paul preached and taught from the pulpit, but tended to keep his distance from the day-to-day goings on of the church. Cliques, outcasts, squabbles, and liaisons; nobody knew those inner church relationships better than Paul's wife, Linda. Rather than preaching, she advised and encouraged from inside the church body. Peter needed to talk to her.

After stopping at home to pick up Zack, Peter headed to Paul and Linda's house. The route took him past the grocery store, a low squat building at the bottom of the hill. He saw several people he remembered arresting the day before. Instead of brawling, they were filling bags with trash and scooping the remnants of eggshells out of the snow and into trash bins. Peter smiled. The town was supporting Tom and, hopefully, their sheriff.

Built with an inheritance from the death of their parents, the parsonage sat in a pretty meadow above Flint Creek on the outskirts of town. The home was built in generous proportions, with a wrap-around porch and windows to match, a sanctuary in any season.

"Is Paul home?" asked Peter when Linda opened the door.

"He's at the church working on his sermon."

"Good. I need to talk to you."

"Oh?"

"About the murders and the church offering theft."

"I've been hoping you would ask," she said as she opened the door wider and stepped aside so Peter could enter. "Tea and cookies?"

"Always."

Peter followed Linda into the kitchen where she loaded a plate with an assortment of Christmas cookies as two cups of tea spun in the microwave.

When they were settled, Peter flipped a cookie to Zack and picked one for himself.

Linda took a sip of her tea before she began. "These are only observations and suspicions. I don't have any real evidence."

"Sure."

"Several months ago, a new couple came to town. From somewhere on the east coast, I think. They were never very specific, which is always a red flag with me. I can't help wondering what they're trying to hide."

"Sometimes people worry about not being welcomed as outsiders."

"True, but this was different. I stood outside and watched as they left one day. Their license plate was covered in mud. I couldn't even tell what state it was from."

Linda, a writer of murder mystery books, was always on the lookout for a crime. She tended to see details overlooked by the general public, which made her a great information source for Peter.

"Just about every car in town has a mud-covered plate in the winter," he observed.

"This was earlier in the fall, before the bad weather started and the only muddy part of the car was the plate."

"Interesting, but hiding where they're from doesn't make them criminals."

"No, but stealing money from the church does."

"So, you think they're the ones who stole the offering money?"

"I do. Jerry, the man, keeps to himself. He stands along the fringes during coffee hour, that sort of thing. He gives me the creeps. I always get the feeling he's casing the joint."

"And the woman?"

"Patty. She's the opposite. Starting the first day, she smooth talked her way onto committees and into positions that normally people have to be here for years to be a part of."

"Like what?"

"Like anything to do with money."

"She was one of the counters when the money went missing," said Peter, recalling the list Paul had given him.

"Yes, she was. Often, newcomers will offer to bring treats for fellowship. Eventually they join the prayer chain and offer to visit the homebound. Patty wasn't interested in any of that, but she's so bubbly and, well, charming, that no one wanted to hear a word against her."

"Manipulative."

"Very. Several women quit speaking to me when I suggested a newcomer shouldn't be put in charge of the money."

"Did anyone else object to Patty being a counter?"

"Alice Celares."

"Did she say why?"

"Not specifically, but I know something happened between them."

"How so?"

"Alice slipped on the ice a while back and broke her wrist. This was before the money went missing. I heard Patty offer to help Alice out with cleaning and things at her house while she healed. Not long after that, they weren't speaking. When the money went missing, Patty actually suggested Alice took the money to frame her."

"Convenient."

"Exactly. Steal the money and then point your finger at the person who suspected you in the first place."

"Weren't there two counters that day."

"There's always two."

"Who was the other one and what does she say?" asked Peter, recalling the other name, but letting Linda tell the story.

"Nadine Ware."

"Old Nadine with the inch-thick lenses who can't see well enough to find her way home?"

"Exactly."

"How did Nadine become a counter?"

"Patty's suggestion. She offered to drive Nadine to and from church, which meant Nadine had to stay until the money was counted anyway."

"Another convenient coincidence. How did Nadine get to church before that?"

"People took turns. Patty volunteering took the burden off everyone else. Nadine lives up Porcupine Creek, out of the way for most people."

"Where do Patty and Jerry live?"

"Not sure. They're secretive about everything. Besides, they haven't been in church since the theft. I wouldn't be surprised if they left town."

"And no one thought that was suspicious?"

Linda shook her head sadly. "We lost half the congregation because of the whole thing. There were the people who stood by Alice and the people who took Patty's side. The Patty people haven't been back."

"Paul didn't mention any of this."

"You know how he is . . . always wanting to believe the best of everyone."

Peter pulled out his copy of the church directory and slid it and a pen over to Linda. "Can you check the names of people who had a beef with Alice?"

"Sure." She opened the book and studied the names. Making a check periodically, she eventually slid the book back to Peter.

He stowed the directory in his vest and pulled out a notebook. "Do you have a last name for Jerry and Patty?"

"Giannetti."

"Jerry and Patty Giannetti. Do you think those are their real names?"

Linda shrugged. "I wouldn't be surprised if someone told me otherwise."

"Description?"

"In their fifties, I would guess. He's kind of beefy, dark hair, trying to hide a bald spot. She's . . . the same, but you don't usually call a woman beefy. Big bust, big hips, big hair. Loud. Draws attention to herself."

"You wouldn't happen to have a picture, would you?"

"Hmmm. Now that you mention it, I might." Linda stood and walked over to the refrigerator. She studied an album worth of photos taped to the side panel and finally pulled one off and carried it back to the table. "Not the greatest, but here's one with both of them at a potluck a month or so ago." Linda pointed to a woman standing in the middle of a group of women, head back in laughter. "Patty." She moved her finger to a man standing alone at the edge of the room. "Jerry. This is typical, her at the center of attention and him in the fringes."

"Can I keep this?" asked Peter.

"Of course. Don't even worry about bringing it back."

"Thanks," he said as he slipped it into his pocket. "What about their car? What does it look like besides muddy plates?"

"Black, late-model Honda. Has a few dings, nothing notable though."

"Don't get your hopes up, but I'll try and track these two down and get your money back."

"Thanks, Peter. That'll go a long way toward mending this church."

Peter put his notebook away, whistled to Zack, and loaded up. Before he left, he pulled out his phone and punched in the number for the sheriff's office.

"Hey, Boss," said Travis when he answered.

"Hey, Travis. Anything interesting going on?"

"Helen's on traffic duty and Angus is on another domestic."

"Anything serious?"

"I don't think so. Mrs. Brady on Ruby Drive claims she can see her next-door neighbor naked when he gets out of his shower."

". . . she's looking through his bathroom window?"

"I guess."

"So, what's her complaint?"

"Not sure. Angus is looking into it." Laughter.

"Can't wait to read that report. Hey, I'm going up Porcupine Creek to visit with Nadine Ware. Could you look into a couple of names for me?"

"Sure. Is this about the murders?"

"No, just a finance issue with the church." He pulled out his notebook. "Jerry and Patty Giannetti. Look for criminal records. Also, if you can find a local address, that would be great."

"On it, Boss."

18

FED BY A spring bubbling to the surface from deep within the Moonlight Mountains, Porcupine Creek turned into a roaring torrent during spring months when winter snows began to melt and spring rains filled every empty gully. During the winter, the stream became a trickle, freezing on the surface to provide easy passage across. Peter was thankful for the county crew who kept the road along the creek open during snowy winter months. Nadine's cottage sat across the creek and up a steep hill. Peter could understand why church folks readily relinquished transport duties to the Giannettis. What he didn't understand was Jerry and Patty's motive, unless it was so Nadine would, literally, turn a blind eye to Patty's theft.

The cottage, built as a retirement home by Nadine's late husband, was small, but well maintained. Peter wondered how the half-blind old woman managed to keep a wood fire going for heat until he spied a propane tank alongside the detached garage. As long as a propane delivery truck could make it to her house, she would stay cozy warm.

Her ears in much better shape than her eyes, Nadine had the door open before Peter was out of his vehicle. "Who's there?" she asked, squinting into the sun.

"Sheriff Elliott, Mrs. Ware."

"Oh, dear. Is everything all right?"

"All good. I just need to ask you a few questions."

"Well, okay. If you have that sweet doggie with you, bring him in. I always keep treats for the doggies."

Peter let Zack out of his kennel compartment and they met Nadine at her door.

"Well, get on in here. We're heating the outside." She led him into a cozy room where two plush armchairs covered in an old-fashioned rose pattern sat in front of an electric fireplace. "Take a load off, Sheriff. I don't imagine you've had much rest since those horrible murders."

A fat corgi, murky-eyed and gray around the muzzle, stood painfully and stiff-legged to greet Zack.

While the dogs sniffed noses, Nadine wandered into another part of the house. While she was gone, Peter studied the walls decorated with an odd assortment of square patches, lighter than the surrounding walls, interspersed among empty wooden frames.

Nadine came back carrying a tea tray with two steaming mugs, a tin of cookies, and two bone-shaped doggie treats. She set the tray on a table between the chairs and gave a treat each to Zack and the corgi.

"I don't bake for myself anymore. Tom stuck these cookies in with my grocery order last week."

"They look delicious," said Peter.

After Nadine settled into her chair, she asked, "So what's this all about, Sheriff?"

"Linda told me about the missing church money."

Nadine jiggled her tea cup, splashing her sweater. "Oh dear. That was unfortunate," she said as she dabbed the spot with a napkin.

"What can you tell me about that day?"

"It was an ordinary Sunday. After services, Patty Giannetti and I counted tithes and then put the bag in the safe."

Peter watched as Nadine leaned closer to the tea table, squinting and feeling her way along until she found the cookie tin. "Is it difficult for you to live here by yourself with your failing eyesight?" he asked.

"Oh, I get by. A woman comes in once a week, and cleans and cooks meals."

"What woman would that be?"

"Mrs. Rice used to come, but Patty's been helping me since she came to town."

Uh, huh, thought Peter. *Helping herself to your treasures.*

"Do you collect paintings?" he asked.

"Oh, yes. Marv didn't trust banks or the stock market. He wanted something he could put his hands on." She glanced vaguely toward the walls and the now empty frames. "That's my retirement."

"How do you manage to count tithing with your limited vision?" asked Peter, steering the subject back to church offerings.

A red flush crawled up Nadine's neck and settled onto her cheeks. "Oh, I don't count. Patty does the counting. Rules say there has to be two, you know."

"So, Patty tells you the total and records it in the book."

"Yes, of course."

"Who puts the money in the bag?"

"Well, Patty does."

"Did you see her put the money in the bag on the day it went missing?"

"Sheriff! Are you suggesting that dear woman would steal from the church?"

"It crossed my mind," he said, glancing at the empty walls. "What do you know about the Giannettis?"

"Well," she paused. "Well, now that I think about it, not much. Jerry's not a talker. Patty's always so interested in my stories, she sits and listens and we laugh—"

"But she's never told you anything about herself?"

"Not really."

"Have they ever mentioned where they came from?"

"No, but they have an east coast accent. You know, New Jersey or somewhere like that."

"Do you know where they live in town?"

"They mention an apartment sometimes."

Finally, thought Peter. *A clue.* Anderson didn't have an abundance of apartments. Narrowing that down should be easy.

He took a cookie for the road and thanked Nadine for her help.

BACK AT THE office, Peter found Angus typing up his report on the domestic call.

"Did you cite Mrs. Brady for peeping or her neighbor for indecent exposure?"

Angus rolled his eyes. "Neither. Mrs. Brady is blind as a bat on a good day. The neighbor's wife recently remodeled the baby's room in a pale pink, including pink curtains. Mrs. Brady saw the pink curtains and assumed it was a pink body. I didn't ask why she decided it was a bathroom window. I suggested she stop looking into windows."

Peter laughed. "Good enough."

Angus quit typing and glanced at Peter. "Hey, Boss..."

"Yeah?"

"I, uh, called Tom yesterday and asked how to get ahold of his brother. I told him we needed to verify information for the investigation."

"Okay."

"Tom told me Bill and Kathy are in Helena visiting their daughter. He gave me the daughter's phone number and address. I called the daughter. She claimed she hasn't seen or talked to her parents in weeks and would have sworn they were at home here in Anderson. She said they keep in touch regularly and hadn't mentioned going on a trip."

"No answer for them on cell phones?"

"Nope. Goes straight to voicemail. I called the sheriff's office in Helena, explained the situation, and asked them to check out the daughter's house. They canvassed several blocks around the house, but didn't find a vehicle belonging to Bill and Kathy Edwards. They said she was completely co-operative and allowed them to search her house and garage without a warrant. Now she's in a panic and wants to file a missing person's report."

"Oh boy. Well, put an APB out on them and their car. They're either on the run or next on the victim list."

"Got it."

"Travis, did you find anything on the Giannettis?" asked Peter.

"Not a Jerry and Patty and definitely not in Anderson. I tried Jeremy, Jerome, Jerold, and Patricia. Nothing."

"Another dead end."

Peter explained about the missing church donations and his visit to Nadine Ware. "I know the murder investigation should be on the top of our list, but I don't want to have to tell Nadine her retirement fund left with the Giannettis."

"A lot of people rent out apartments in their houses," said Angus. "Basements, studios over garages, that sort of thing."

"Where can we get a list?" asked Peter, looking at Travis.

"Mabel," he turned and picked up the receiver on his desk phone. "I should put her on speed dial."

Ancient Mabel managed the Anderson Chamber of Commerce without the handicaps of modern technology. Volumes of decades-old binders overflowing with yellowed, crumbling pages covered every shelf in her office. File cabinets held treasures more befitting to the historical society. The clutter was deceiving. Mabel knew every volume from beginning to end and not a morsel of gossip happened in the Anderson business community without Mabel's knowledge.

"Hi, Mabel," said Travis in a friendly tone when she answered the phone.

"Travis? What are you pestering me about now?"

"It's been weeks, Mabel. How've you been?"

"Every day is one day closer to the end . . ."

Travis pictured Mabel with her shapeless gray helmet of hair and old-fashioned half-moon glasses hanging from a beaded string. "Are you going to retire?" he asked.

"Retire?" she snorted with laughter, ending in a hacking cough. "Not before I die. What d'ya want anyway?"

"A list of apartments in town."

"For heaven's sake, Travis. There's only two apartment buildings in Anderson. What d'ya need a list for?"

"Not those, Mabel. I need a list of private apartments. You know, in houses or garages."

Travis waited as Mabel paused, anticipating her answer.

"Y'know, Travis, it could be now and then folks rent out a room unofficial like."

"Exactly. Could you make me a list?"

"Is this a sting operation? Are you cracking down on slum lords?"

Smothering a giggle, Travis said, "No, Mabel, we're looking for crime suspects."

"Crime, huh? What sort of crime?"

"It's an ongoing investigation. I can't say."

"So real hush, hush then?"

"Sure."

"Well, as long as you don't tell anyone where you got the information—"

"Cross my heart."

Travis disconnected. "She'll have it ready in twenty minutes," he said to Peter and Angus.

"Great," said Peter. "Angus can pick up the list and start checking out apartments."

Travis cleared his throat. "Y'know, those apartments on Summit would be a good place to look."

"Isn't that where Birdie lives?" asked Angus.

"Uh . . . yeah."

"Will you be seeing Birdie?" asked Peter.

A blush creeped onto Travis's cheeks. "I could . . . I mean if you need me to."

"Go ahead. Ask Birdie if she's seen anyone who fits the description of the Giannettis or their car. Oh, yeah—" Peter pulled the picture of Patty and Jerry out of his pocket and handed it to Travis. "Make a few copies of this. It should help with identification."

Hoping for a private conversation with Birdie, Travis waited patiently while Angus gathered his gear and headed across the street to Mabel's office.

"I'm going over to Tony Celares's house," said Peter, after Angus left. "He's had a few days to think about things. He may have a few ideas why someone would murder his parents."

"Okay, Boss," said Travis, finger already poised over the speed-dial button to Birdie's number.

19

RINGING THE DOORBELL at Tony's house proved to be futile, as did rapping the lion's head door knocker. Peter doubted Tony and Susan left town in the midst of planning a funeral but the curtains were drawn and no lights showed along the edges.

He got back into his vehicle and drove to the bank. Rather than going inside, he went to the drive-up window.

"Hi, Sheriff," said a pretty young teller.

"Hey, Sissy. Is Tony in today?"

"Naw. He's out this week on account of his parents." She glanced down in deference to the deceased.

"Okay, thanks," said Peter. He waved and pulled into the bank parking lot, stopped, thought for minute, and drove back around to the drive-up window.

"Hey, Sissy, you wouldn't happen to have Tony's phone number handy, would you?"

"Well, we don't normally give that out, but since it's you . . ." Sissy glanced at what Peter assumed was a list on the wall inside her teller's window, wrote a number on a piece of paper, and sent it out through the window drawer.

"Thanks. I appreciate it."

He pulled into the parking lot, parked, and punched Tony's number into his phone. The call went straight to voice mail. Peter left a message for Tony to call when he was available.

＊＊＊

THE GATEWAY TO Eternal Rest funeral parlor was conveniently located on a side street around the corner from the Stone County Hospital. In his role as sheriff, Peter often found himself in the basement processing rooms, enduring the acidic stink of embalming fluid. Today, he entered through the front doors. Mortician Lee Garnet, dressed as ever in an immaculate black suit and garnet red tie, greeted Peter.

"Sheriff," he said holding out a perfectly manicured hand. "What brings you in today?"

"I'm looking for Tony and Susan Celares. Have you seen them?"

"No, actually. I prepared a presentation of funeral options in anticipation of their visit, but they haven't been in." His forehead furrowed with worry. "Do you suppose they chose to use an out-of-town parlor?"

"I don't know why they would, Lee. You have an excellent reputation." Peter pulled out a card. "Give me a call if you see them."

Back in his vehicle, Peter considered his options. As far as he knew, Susan didn't work outside the home. Other than the country club, he didn't have an outside connection for her, so he drove to the club, told Zack he would be back soon, and went inside.

Strong odors of pine, perfume, and booze hung in the air. The Christmas tree and most of the décor from the Christmas gala remained. A lone woman stood on a ladder at the edge of the room, mop of gray hair dusted with cobwebs, pulling strings of garland from walls and ceiling. She looked down when she heard the door open and close.

"Sorry, Sheriff, the party's over. All the hooligans went home."

Peter laughed. "Hello, Anne. I'm sure none of the country club set would appreciate being called hooligans."

"Probably not, but I'm short on goodwill after the Christmas gala. Everyone's excited about decorating beforehand, but afterwards . . ."

As she climbed down the ladder, Peter glanced out the window overlooking the parking lot and watched a man jogging to a silver-hued luxury sedan while casting furtive looks toward the building.

"Who's that?" he asked.

They stood and watched as the man fumbled with his key fob, wrenched the car door open, and tumbled into his seat. Tires squealed and slid across the ice as he peeled out of the parking lot.

"Craig Schlepp. Strange. He was in the office going over the board meeting schedule when I came in. I wonder what he's in such a hurry for."

"Me too. What's his position here?"

"Chairman of the board. The big guy himself."

"Hmm," Peter rubbed his chin. "You wouldn't happen to have his address and phone number handy?"

"Sure. We don't usually give out that information, but since it's you . . ." She led him to a back office, studied a member list pinned to a bulletin board and pointed to Craig Schlepp. "Do you need me to write it down?"

"Yes, thanks."

Anne tore a page from a notebook on the desk, wrote down the information, and handed the paper to Peter. She added her own number for good measure. Peter folded the paper and slipped it into his coat pocket.

"I'm pretty sure you didn't come here for Craig Schlepp's phone number, Sheriff. Did you need something else?"

"Yeah. I stopped by the Celareses' house and nobody was home. Would you know where I could find them?"

"Susan shows up here occasionally, but I haven't seen Tony . . . well, probably since the end of golf season."

"What can you tell me about them? Any thoughts about who would murder Tony's parents?"

"I'm more familiar with Susan than Tony. The country club is her thing. He golfs with friends now and then, but isn't part of the men's league. I think there's a medical issue that keeps him from playing regularly."

"Gout."

"Gout?"

"Yeah, he has a gout problem."

"Ooooh, I hear that can be painful."

"Any thoughts on the state of their marriage?"

"I don't like to gossip."

"It's not gossip during an investigation."

"Um, okay. I've never heard either one say a bad word about the other."

"Infidelities?"

"Not that I know of, but . . ."

"But?"

"Well, lately she and Craig, the man you saw scurrying out of here . . . lately, I've seen them huddled together, deep in conversation. It's always at odd hours when the club is closed."

"An affair?"

"No. I can usually peg the affairs. The eye contact and sly smiles across the room. Subtle touching. Showing up at the clubhouse at the same time and without their spouses. I've been managing this place for so long, I'm part of the woodwork. People don't notice me noticing."

"If not an affair, then what?"

"Not sure. If they were on a committee together, I would say they're planning an event. This is more like plotting."

"Did you ever overhear their conversation?"

"Unlike the lovers, they're real careful."

"How about woman friends? Does Susan have a BFF?"

"Not that I know of. This group of women split and make up so often I can't keep track."

Peter thanked Anne. "If you think of anything else, give me a call."

He left the club and drove past the Celareses' house, hoping to see fresh signs that someone was home. Lights glowed through the windows of neighboring houses, combating the early gloom of winter evenings, but the Celareses' home remained dark.

Peter pulled up to the curb. "Stay here, Zack," he said as he took a flashlight out of his duty vest. He stepped into the night, his stomach rumbling with the aroma of many dinners wafting through the neighborhood. Food could wait. Concern about Tony and Susan came first.

Peter made his way around the side of the house, watching for unusual footprints and signs of suspicious activity. Tracks from two cars showed several passes in and out of a detached garage, but a lack of windows prevented Peter from seeing if one or both cars were missing. Around the rear of the house, a covered porch sheltered the back door. The door hung open, banging against the side of the house. On the steps and into the yard, dark splotches interspersed with gaping footprints stained the snow on the edges of Peter's flashlight beam. As he moved closer, the splotches turned red. Drag marks smeared with red ended at tire tracks where a vehicle had backed into the yard from the alley.

Peter took out his phone and punched in Helen's number. "What are you doing?" he asked.

"Eating dinner. What's going on?"

"I'm at Tony Celares's place. Nobody has seen him or his wife for a while and there's blood streaks coming out the back door."

"I'll be right there."

<hr>

HALF DELIRIOUS WITH hunger and thirst, Tony dreamed of an extra-large supreme pizza and a tall glass of beer . . . and a bottle of painkillers.

He thought of Susan and wondered if she felt the same discomforts. Was she hurt? Susan. He truly loved Susan in spite of herself and felt guilty for not being able to give her the life she wanted. He bargained with God. *If you let me see her again, I'll be better. A better husband. A better human being.*

The garage entry door opened and he cringed, expecting kicks to his already bruised ribs.

"Sit up," said the voice, quieter, conversational.

He pushed himself up as well as he could and felt hands assist. His abductor released his gag and the zip tie around his wrists. He felt cold plastic against his hands. A water bottle.

"Open up. These should help with your pain."

He opened his mouth and felt dry tablets drop onto his tongue. Rather than relief, he felt apprehension. From bully to friend, he knew the technique. His abductor would attempt to ease information out of Tony that he didn't have.

"Drink as much as you want," said the Voice, as Tony chugged water from the bottle. "Do you need to use the bathroom?"

Tony nodded and eased his aching muscles into standing. His abductor led him to the bathroom across the floor.

Thirst quenched, bladder emptied, and pain relief on the way, Tony decided to push his luck. "Could I have something to eat?"

The Voice paused and led Tony back to his mat on the floor. "Sit there. Don't move!"

Tony heard footstep cross the floor and then back, followed by the crackle of snack paper. A sticky rectangle dropped onto his hand.

"Granola bar. That's all I have."

Tony heard the sounds of dragging against cement and then the unfolding of a metal chair. His abductor sat and patiently waited while Tony finished chewing.

"I understand," said the Voice, "why you wouldn't want to tell me where your parents hid the stuff. There's a lot of money involved. You're thinking you'll tell me and then I'll go get it and leave you here to die."

"Am I wrong? Where's Susan," his voice cracked. "Is she still alive?"

"I'll make a deal with you. You tell me where it's hidden and I'll give you a cut."

"Susan first. Prove she's okay or I won't deal."

Tony felt a cold metal circle against the back of his head. A gun.

"That's NOT going to happen!" said the Voice. "I'm running out of patience with you. Where is it?"

"I. Don't. Know."

Tony felt the gag wrap back around his mouth, tighter than before. "Put your hands together. Tight!"

Zip ties, once bearable, now cut into his skin. A few swift kicks to his ribs reminded him who was in charge. The door slammed shut and Tony was once more alone.

20

OLICE ACADEMY AND a degree in criminal justice under his belt, Travis checked all the boxes required for law enforcement. What he lacked was the temperament. Gore left him gagging and violence baffled his friendly nature. In spite of that, he relished a chance to polish his investigative skills, even if unofficially. Investigation was his excuse for a dinner meeting with Deputy Birdie Bradshaw.

Travis rushed home to prepare for his date. He considered clothing options, but reminded himself it wasn't an official date. Since Birdie's night shift would begin directly after dinner, she would be in her deputy uniform. Travis took a clean and pressed button-down shirt out of his closet. Fresh jeans would do. He combed his hair and shaved and contemplated what it would take to win Birdie's heart.

Birdie arrived early to the Silver Dollar Saloon, Anderson's version of an elegant steak house. Original brick walls, tin ceilings, and leather seating carefully oiled through many decades provided an ambience that leaned toward elegance. Weary travelers, tourists, and locals missed that cue. Fine dining attire consisted of clean blue jeans and shirts with all their buttons. Birdie fit in with her deputy uniform. She ignored the menu, and ordered the nightly special for both her and Travis.

Travis rushed in late, face lighting up when he saw Birdie. "Sorry I'm late. Mabel called and it's hard to make that a fast conversation."

"Mabel from the Chamber of Commerce?"

"Yeah. I asked her for information on local apartments. She thought of a few more." He explained about Patty and Jerry and the missing church funds.

"So, you're wondering if I've seen anyone who fits their description?" asked Birdie.

"Well, yeah, but mostly in your apartment complex."

Birdie thought for a bit. "No. Not around my place, but there's not a lot of turn-around. Most everyone has been there a long time . . . longer than me."

The waitress brought their food and they concentrated on eating. After a while Birdie said, "You like investigation, huh?"

"Yeah. I like finding clues and solving puzzles."

An awkward silence followed, both knowing the unspoken: Travis could never be a real deputy.

"Hey," said Birdie, "How about riding around with me for a while tonight? We could drive by those apartments Mabel mentioned."

"Really?"

"I'll check with Peter first." She punched in Peter's number and relayed her request. "He says okay but not to let you get into any trouble."

Travis laughed. "I won't get in your way?"

"No way. I get bored driving around by myself all night. Hardly anything happens until the bars close."

<hr>

THE CONVERTED GARAGE had no number, but judging from the houses on either side, it fit the address noted in Mabel's shaky handwriting. Birdie slowed to crawl as she and Travis searched for signs of habitation.

"How many addresses did Mabel come up with?" asked Birdie.

"Not sure. Angus picked up the first list. These are extras she thought about later."

"What are we supposed to do if we find them?"

"Let Peter know. There's no proof they did anything wrong at this point."

"There aren't any tracks in the snow. Next?"

Travis rattled off an address ending in 'one-quarter'."

"One-quarter? What kind of address is one-quarter?"

"Two apartments in a garage? I don't know. Let's find out."

<hr>

ON THE FAR edge of town, an enterprising landowner with a roomy yard had installed a pre-fab cabin with its own address and alley entrance. Lights filtered through heavy curtains and a snow shovel leaned against the cabin next to the door.

"236 and a quarter. Makes sense now," said Birdie, as she stopped and studied a black car parked next to the cabin. "Is that a Honda?"

"I can't tell from here. Too dark and too much snow." Travis started to open the door.

"Sit tight. You so much as slip on the ice while riding around with me and I'm toast."

Travis laughed, "Good point."

Birdie had no sooner turned her flashlight beam onto the back of the car when the cabin door flew open. A large, brassy woman grabbed the snow shovel and, brandishing it as a club, barreled down the path.

"Sheriff's department," yelled Birdie. "Stop right there."

Without slowing down, the woman continued toward Birdie. "What do you think you're doing messing around my car!"

Travis leaped out of the patrol vehicle and threw himself between Birdie and Patty. The shovel hit Travis full in the face, cracking his nose and knocking him to the ground. Blood gushed onto his coat and splattered the snow.

Birdie pulled a taser out of her duty belt, zapping the woman before she could get in another swing. The woman shrieked in pain, her body dropping to the ground as muscle contractions rendered her unable to move. Assailant subdued, Birdie snapped on handcuffs, took a deep breath to collect herself, and hurried to Travis's side.

21

PETER MET HELEN in front of the Celareses' house. She grabbed the crime scene kit out of her vehicle as well as a bulging plastic grocery bag.

Handing Peter the bag, she said, "I figured you wouldn't get dinner."

"Thanks!" Peter opened the bag and found two sandwiches wrapped in plastic, a bag of potato chips, and a can of pop.

"It's only peanut butter and jelly, but it'll get you through."

"You're the best, Helen." He unwrapped one of the sandwiches and wolfed it down, followed by the pop. Stomach appeased, he stowed the rest of the food in his vest for later.

Pointing his flashlight along his previous footprints, Peter led Helen to the back of the house and lit up the stained snow.

"Looks like blood to me," she said, digging in her kit for a bottle of luminol.

As Helen aimed her spray bottle toward the splotch, Peter switched off his flashlight. In the pitch black of the backyard, a blue glow confirmed their suspicions. Blood.

"Human?" asked Helen.

"That's my guess. Let's check out the house."

Prepared for any sort of surprise, Peter and Helen entered through the back door. A runner rug muffled their footsteps as they crept close to the wall. In the beam of Peter's flashlight, red streaks and splotches stained the light blue rug covering the floor.

The streaks continued through the kitchen, and to the front door where they ended in a pool of congealed blood.

"Ground zero," said Helen.

"Looks like it."

"One pool of blood, one body. Tony or Susan?"

"Or someone else." Peter led the way through the rest of the main floor and up a stairway of pristine carpeting.

Bedrooms, bathrooms, office, and closets were clear of blood and bodies, dead or alive. They returned to the first floor where they found another stairway leading to an unfinished basement.

"I don't think I've ever seen a basement so clean," said Helen.

Peter high-beamed the flashlight around the room, concentrating on the cement floor. "Yeah, weird. Like someone trying to cover up a crime scene," said Peter, with visions of a serial basement killer floating through his head.

"Down here, but not upstairs?"

"Probably not, but give the floor a few squirts of luminol just in case."

He turned off the flashlight while Helen aimed a sweeping spray across the floor and up the stairway. Nothing.

"No blood or bodies down here." Peter turned the flashlight on and they made their way up the stairs.

He found a light switch by the front door and flipped it on. "After we process the scene, I'll bring Zack in. If the blood's from Tony or Susan, he'll let us know."

While Helen took photographs and samples, Peter studied a key rack by the back door. Several single keys on plastic tags caught his eye; he lifted one labeled 'garage' off its hook. A pool of blood and a missing body justified entering the garage without a warrant. The labeled key simplified things.

Placing his ear as close as he dared to the frosty metal garage door, Peter listened for sound. Weather stripping around the door prevented light from filtering through. Everything quiet, he stood to the side of the door, slipped the key into the lock, knocked, and announced, "Sheriff Elliott. I'm coming in."

A dirty maroon pickup truck sat on the far side of the garage, with the assorted trappings of life stacked along the edges. Frozen tire tracks in the closest stall showed signs of recent occupancy. Peter used the high beam of his flashlight to expose every nook and cranny of the room and underneath the truck. Like the house basement, the garage was surprisingly tidy.

The truck, cold to the touch, was unlocked. Peter searched the interior for signs of an altercation or trauma. Nothing.

"Only one vehicle in the garage," he said to Helen, when back in the house. "A pickup truck. The paperwork has both of their names, but I'm thinking Tony is the main driver. Susan doesn't strike me as the pickup truck type. Find anything interesting in here?"

"The murder weapon." She smiled and held up a full wine bottle, matted sand colored hair and blood caked on one side.

"Hmmm, not a typical choice of weapon for an intruder. An act of passion?"

"If you were standing around with a wine bottle and lost your temper. Looks to me like whoever did this waited for the victim at the door. He comes in, closes the door, and wham. Lights out."

"He or she. Tony and Susan are both blond." Peter studied the layout of the house. A short wall separated the entryway from the living room. "The victim wouldn't see someone standing around this corner as he came in the door. Still . . . a wine bottle?"

"I'm finished here if you want to bring Zack in," said Helen.

"Sure. Find a piece of clothing each for Tony and Susan. Something they wore recently."

"Already done." Helen held up a brown men's T-shirt and flowery woman's blouse. "I got them out of the dirty clothes so they should be well-scented."

"Perfect!"

Avoiding the bloody front hallway, Peter went out through the back door and let Zack out of his kennel compartment. He fastened on a trailing harness attached to a thirty-foot rolled bull hide lead, and said, "Let's go, Zack."

"Who should we do first?" asked Helen when they came in the back door.

"Start with Tony. His truck's in the garage."

Helen handed the T-shirt to Peter, who held it under Zack's nose. "Find, Zack."

Zack sniffed, wandered in and out of the kitchen, and started to go into other rooms. Tony's scent permeated every part of the house. Peter tightened the lead and brought Zack into the front hallway, close to the blood.

He again put the shirt under Zack's nose. "Find."

This time, Zack concentrated on the blood scent and led Peter down the back hallway, through the kitchen, and out the back door. He followed blood smears across the backyard to where they ended at tire tracks. He sniffed to the alley and walked in both directions trying to pick up the scent. Sniffing complete, he sat and looked at Peter.

"Can we assume someone whacked Tony on the head, dragged his body through the house, and put him in a car?" asked Helen.

"Or, Tony dragged the body. Dogs will generally pick up the freshest scent, but Zack can't specify if Tony was the body or the one doing the dragging."

"Wow, you're right."

"Number one rule, don't assume. Let's see what Zack does with Susan's shirt."

They went back into the front hallway. Peter held Susan's blouse under Zack's nose and said, "Find."

Zack ignored the blood. He wandered into the living room to one end of the couch. A stack of decorating books covered most of an end table and an abandoned coffee cup sat on the nearby coffee table.

"Where Susan usually sits," observed Helen.

"Yep." Peter held the blouse under Zack's nose again and said, "Find."

Zack wandered through various rooms of the house, all permeated with Susan's scent. He led Peter through the back hallway, out the door, to the garage, and back to the house.

"This tells us nothing except she lives here and parks her car in the garage," said Peter.

"But where is Susan and was she a part of whatever happened here?" asked Helen.

"No idea. Can you get anything from the footprints in the backyard?"

They went out to the backyard. Helen made her way along the edge of the footprints, careful not to disturb evidence.

With her flashlight on wide beam, she studied the prints. "Doubtful I can get anything from these or the tire tracks. Fresh deep powder caves in on itself, covering everything. The heavy body dragged past added more on top of that."

"More questions than answers," said Peter. "We need to find Susan and Tony and figure out who that blood belongs to." He glanced at Helen's weary face. "Go home and get some rest. We have a big day ahead of us tomorrow. I'll take care of things tonight."

After Helen left, Peter punched in the number for the sheriff's office.

"Hey, Peter, what's up?" asked Debbie when she answered the phone.

"Hey, Debbie, would you find registrations for all vehicles owned by Susan or Tony Celares?"

"Sure. Anything else?"

"Yeah, also a vehicle registration for Craig Schlepp."

"Will do."

"Thanks, Debbie."

Peter disconnected, punched in the number for the county hospital emergency room, and asked for the charge nurse.

"Nurse Kelly, can I help you?"

"Hi, Kelly. It's Peter Elliott. I'm looking for a possible assault victim. Have you had anyone come in with a nasty head wound?"

"Only Travis, your office clerk."

"What?!"

"He's here now. Birdie brought him in . . . he'll be okay, just a broken nose."

"Oh, boy. Tell them I'll be right there."

22

"I TOLD HIM TO stay in the vehicle," said Birdie when she met Peter in the parking lot. "On the other hand, if he hadn't run between me and the shovel, I would be sitting in there with a broken nose."

"No worries. This one's on Travis." He nodded toward her Explorer. "So, who's our perp?"

"Not sure. She didn't have ID."

"Did you ask her?"

"She's not talking."

"Okay. Bring her in and book her. I'll take care of Travis."

Nose swollen and clothes covered in blood, Travis sat, triumphant, on the edge of the emergency room cot.

"Birdie's okay, though, that's what counts," he said to Peter's question of why Travis had left the patrol vehicle.

"You're . . . a . . . you're okay with all this? Not stressed or anything?"

"I feel great! I saved Birdie."

TRAVIS HOME SAFE, Peter drove to the sheriff's office and found Debbie hunched, fear in her eyes, behind the office desk. Birdie, hand on taser, prepared for a possible assault. A beefy man with dark hair and a bad comb-over stood too close, spewing vitriol and threats.

"What's going on?" asked Peter, walking past the man and standing next to Birdie. Zack followed Peter, a low growl in his throat.

"This is Mr. Jerry Giannetti. Apparently, our prisoner is Patty Giannetti. He's demanding her release."

Jerry continued his rant. Ignoring him, Peter turned to Birdie. "Have you typed up the arrest report?"

"Uh . . . no, not yet."

"Go ahead and type your report. I'll deal with Mr. Giannetti." He turned to Jerry. "Mr. Giannetti, you will lower your voice and speak in a respectful manner or I will be forced to physically remove you from the premises."

"You and who else?!" shouted Jerry, stepping closer to Peter and raising his fist.

An electric crackle followed by a scream filled the room as Jerry slumped to the floor. Peter bent and snapped handcuffs around Jerry's thick wrists.

"Help me get him into a cell."

Stunned into submission, Jerry allowed Peter and Birdie, one on each arm, to lead him into a cell and drop him on a cot. He scowled, silent as he watched them leave, closing and locking the door behind them.

Birdie gave Debbie a thumbs-up as she followed Peter to his office, dropping with exhaustion into a comfy leather chair.

"Tell me what happened tonight," he said.

She relayed the story of finding the pre-fab cabin and getting out to check to see if the car was a Honda. "Things went downhill pretty fast from there."

"So, the attack was unprovoked."

"No question about that. We were parked in the alley . . . public property, and I hadn't even touched the car when this woman—Patty Giannetti—came running at me with the shovel."

"Did she know you're a deputy?"

"Definitely. I identified myself as from the sheriff's office. She didn't even slow down."

"Did you get anything out of her after you brought her in?"

"Nothing. She asked for her phone call and didn't say another word until Jerry showed up."

"No explanation for the attack then?"

"None. She didn't want us anywhere near the car though, which makes me wonder what she had to hide."

Peter looked at his watch. "We'll need more evidence than suspicion before Judge Knowles will issue a search warrant. Drive by, check out the car, and run the plates. If I'm right about Patty stealing paintings from Nadine Ware, the evidence may be stored in that car."

"Will do." Birdie smiled, thrilled to be doing something besides drunk patrol.

Peter called into the outer office, "Debbie, were you able to find the vehicle information for the Celareses and Craig Schlepp?"

"Sure did." She walked into the office and handed him a thin stack of papers. "Two for the Celareses and two for Craig Schlepp."

Peter scanned the papers. Handing one to Birdie, he said, "The Celareses' red truck is in the garage, but this one is missing. A sapphire blue Buick Encore. Funny, I had her pegged as a Cadillac girl."

"A wannabee maybe."

He handed her two more sheets. "Craig Schlepp's vehicles. A white Ford truck and a silver sedan."

"Who's Craig Schlepp and how does he figure in all this?"

"The chairman of the board at the country club. He and Susan Celares have something going on."

"An affair?"

"Anne at the club didn't think so, but Susan is missing and Craig was acting spooked when I was at the club. Drive by and check out his house."

"Is it too late to knock on the door?"

"Not if someone's home. We've got a possible homicide and two missing people. Craig is a person of interest. If Susan and Craig's vehicles aren't at his house, put out an APB for them and their vehicles."

He whistled for Zack. "I'm going home to get a little shut-eye. Keep me posted on what you find."

"Got it." She followed him out the door and to the parking lot.

⸻⬥⬥⬥⸻

FLASHLIGHT ON HIGH beam, Birdie peered into the windows of Giannettis' black Honda. The typical detritus of car living, candy wrappers and drink cups, cluttered the console and floor of the front seat. The middle seat was surprisingly bare, except for thin, bubble wrapped squares and rectangles.

Bingo! Stolen paintings.

Birdie walked around to the rear and noted cardboard boxes jammed into the cargo area of the small car.

More stolen goods?

She used snow to wash away mud from the license plate, took down the number, and sent it to Debbie.

CRAIG SCHLEPP'S HOUSE sat on a two-acre lot in a newer subdivision at the north end of town. The modern design, consisting of a tall rectangle topped with a sloping roof on one side and all windows on the other, spoke of city money moving into the countryside. The light from a single bulb shone from a side window, a nightlight in an otherwise dark house.

A two-stall garage set under the living space made up the lower level, with windows set in the doors to complement the overall house design. Flashlight beam set on narrow, Birdie walked up the driveway and peered through the garage windows. Both stalls were occupied, each with a vehicle described in Craig's registration reports. Other than Birdie's patrol vehicle, the surrounding streets were clear. If Susan Celares was here, she didn't come in her own vehicle.

Birdie walked around to the front of the house and pushed the doorbell button. Inside, a short burst of chimes rang through the house. She waited, listening for movement. Several minutes went by before she heard a thumping on stairs and a sleep-graveled voice.

"Who's there? What do you want?" An eye peeked through slats of blinds covering the glass door.

Birdie held up her badge. "Stone County Sheriff's Department."

The eyes in the window grew wide and frightened as they registered the uniform and badge. Moments passed before the door opened a crack.

"Mr. Schlepp?" asked Birdie. "Craig Schlepp?"

"Yeah."

"I need to ask you a few questions. May I come in?"

The door opened fully. "What's this about?"

"Susan and Tony Celares."

"From the country club? What about them?"

"They're missing. Can we sit down?"

"Missing?" asked Craig, with a note of worry. He pulled his lush robe closer and stepped aside to let Birdie pass. Closing the door, he led her into a sitting area in the wide-open floor plan.

Reverting to deeply-ingrained manners, he asked, "Would you care for something to drink? Coffee? Water?"

"No, thank you. I have a few questions. It shouldn't take long," She sat in an upholstered straight-backed chair that proved to be more comfortable than it looked.

"So, Susan and Tony Celares are missing," said Craig, dropping into an easy chair. "What does this have to do with me?"

"How well do you know the Celareses?"

"They're members of the country club. I'm chairman of the board."

"What's your relationship with Susan? We were told you're close."

"Close? Like an affair? No way. She's kind of a cold fish if you ask me. Who said we were close?"

Birdie ignored his question and watched a bead of sweat run down the side of his face. "Were you working on any projects together?"

"We recently held our Christmas gala. Susan's always in charge of that and runs the plans by me."

"Nothing outside the club?"

He wiped away the sweat. "Uh . . . no."

"And Tony? How well do you know him?"

"He's not around much. Comes in for a round of golf now and then."

"Did you know his parents?"

"Tony's parents? No. Heard about that bus accident last fall, though, and their murders." He shook his head. "Tragic."

Standing to leave, Birdie handed Craig a card. "If you think of anything that could help us find the Celareses, please let me know as soon as possible."

Craig saw Birdie to the door and watched as she drove away. He retrieved his phone from the bedside table, punched in a familiar number, and listened as the call went straight to voice mail.

"This has gone too far, Susan. Call me."

23

"BAR FIGHT?" ASKED Angus, taking in Travis's black eyes and swollen nose when he walked into the sheriff's office the next morning.

"He jumped between Birdie and a shovel," said Peter, coming in behind Travis.

"How'd that happen?" asked Helen.

Travis described the incident with Patty Giannetti.

"Way to go, Travis!" said Helen, giving him a wink. "I'll bet Birdie is grateful."

Travis blushed around the edges of his bruises.

"You don't need to be here today," said Peter. "A broken nose warrants a sick day or two."

"I'd rather be here than sitting at home with ice on my face. Besides, it looks worse than it feels."

Zack's nose sniffed along the edge of Travis's desk and Helen said, "You forgot the donuts."

"Tom didn't get his delivery at the store this morning. No donuts."

Peter rolled his eyes. "We can survive one morning without donuts."

Sad puppy-dog eyes from both Zack and Helen changed his mind. "We have to order in breakfast for the prisoners anyway. Will you settle for farmer's omelets from Dixie's?"

"Yeah!" said the crew in unison. Zack wagged his tail and drooled.

While they waited for delivery, the crew followed Peter into his office and settled in for an update of the current cases.

"First, the Celareses' murders," said Peter. "Anything new on evidence from the house?"

"Nothing significant," said Helen. "Clem went through the fingerprints and compared them to family and friends. They all checked out."

"I've been through the computer files," said Travis. "Nothing new there."

"On the bus accident motive, any new thoughts on Angela Brown, Angus?"

"She lied about leaving the house during the time of the murders. Other than that, no."

"Couldn't hurt to confront her about that lie, and plan another stakeout. Find out where she goes when she thinks nobody is watching."

"Will do."

"Any leads on Bill and Kathy Edwards?"

"Nothing on the APB. I talked to Tom this morning. He's a wreck. He swears they told him they were spending Christmas in Helena, but . . ."

"But?"

"Like I said, he's pretty shook up. Apparently, the friendship between Kathy and the Celareses was all an act."

"Not Bill?" asked Helen.

"Bill didn't blame Frank for the accident. Kathy did. Tom suspects she was behind the rumors saying he was drunk."

"Was she mad enough to kill?"

"Could be. She went through all the lawyers in Missoula trying to sue Frank for wrongful death. Nobody would take the case when they saw the accident reports. She's been, well, out for blood ever since. Tom thinks she and Bill are headed for a divorce."

"It wouldn't be the first time a child's death broke up a marriage," said Helen.

"Let me know as soon as we get a hit on that APB. Next . . . we haven't discussed Tony and Susan as possible murderers," said Peter. "What would be their motive for murdering his parents?"

"Money," said Helen. "Frank and Alice had a nice nest egg built up for retirement. Maybe they weren't dying fast enough for the heirs."

"I did find a will," added Travis. "Tony inherits every-thing."

"But not Susan?" asked Helen.

"Susan only if Tony dies before his parents."

"Giving Susan a motive for killing Tony."

Peter filled Angus and Travis in on the missing Tony and Susan and the blood trail through their house. "One of the vehicles, a blue Buick, is also missing."

"Coincidence that this happened right after his parents' murder?" asked Angus. "Whoever killed Frank and Alice may have murdered Tony and Susan."

"Motive?"

"Revenge for the kids' death? 'You killed my son so I'll kill yours'?"

"According to Zack's nose," said Peter, "Tony either dragged the body through his house or was the body. Susan wasn't a part of that."

"Accomplice?" asked Angus. "Susan hires someone to murder Tony and that someone drags his body through the house?"

"Which brings us to Craig Schlepp," said Peter. "Anne at the country club said Craig and Susan have been 'plotting' together about something. Birdie questioned Craig last night. She said he was nervous, but denied having anything to do with Susan other than planning the Christmas gala."

"What would be Craig's motive for helping Susan with a murder?" asked Helen. "Are they in a relationship?"

"Not according to Anne, and Craig denied it when Birdie asked."

"Could Zack do his sniffing magic with Craig's scent at Tony's house?" asked Angus.

"We need to rule him out," said Peter. "I'll stop by today and pick up a piece of clothing. Moving on from that, suppose Tony murdered someone in his house. Any thoughts on victim or motive?"

"Tony murdered his parents, someone found out, and is blackmailing him?" asked Helen.

A knock on the door made them jump. Travis, closest to the door, opened it for a delivery driver with a bag full of take-out boxes.

Travis distributed meals to the crew, emptied the contents of a box specifically labeled 'Zack' into a food dish by Peter's desk, and brought the last two meals downstairs to the Giannettis in their cells.

Opening his box, Peter found a note that said, 'call me,' signed by Dixie. He smiled and slipped the note into his pocket as a reminder for later.

After a moment of silence while everyone curbed their hunger, Peter asked, "Any hits on those APBs for the Celareses and their car?"

"Nothing yet," said Travis

"Dang. Next case. The Giannettis' car came back registered in the name of Gerold and Priscilla Giannetti."

"Aah, a slight first name change keeps them under the radar," said Travis. "That's why they didn't show up on my searches."

"Exactly. Jerry is Gerry with a G and Patty is Prissy."

"I don't blame her," said Helen. "I'd rather be a Patty than a Prissy."

"A rose by any other name and all that, but these two are more like weeds. Patty has multiple arrest warrants out of several states."

"Let me guess," said Helen, "theft?"

"Yep. Frequent and widespread." Peter told them about Birdie's suspicions of paintings in the back seats.

"What about Jerry?" asked Angus.

"No active warrants for him."

"Weird. He stands on the sidelines and lets Patty do the dirty work," observed Helen.

"Judge Knowles approved a search warrant for the Giannetti car and rented cabin," said Peter. "Angus, you can check those out. If you find evidence of theft from the church, Nadine Ware, or anyone else, we'll pursue charges."

"On it."

"Helen . . ."

"Yeah?"

"I have a special assignment for you."

"Oh boy."

"It involves a whole lot of Baptist women and fine home cooking."

Helen perked up. "Do tell."

"Paul says there's a potluck tonight at the church. It's an attempt at reconciling the pro-Patty and pro-Alice factions. Everyone is invited and encouraged to forgive and forget. Now that Patty—Prissy—is in jail, her supporters are rethinking their position."

"Is this about the murder or the missing money?"

"Both. The money is an issue, but someone left the note on the church door. We don't know for sure if it was about Alice, but it's a small town. The murderer could be from the church. I want you two at the potluck, civilian clothing. Listen. Ask questions. Get people talking."

"Unofficial like."

"Yeah. I'll be there, too, as the pastor's brother. But, I can't cover everyone. It'll be less suspicious if a woman covers the women."

"Sure. It beats traffic duty."

"Good. Everyone have their assignments?"

"Yep."

The crew finished their breakfasts and headed out the door. Office empty, Peter picked up his phone and punched in a number.

"Hey, Peter," said Dixie. "You got my note."

"I did."

"Are you calling to ask me to go on a stakeout?"

"No, even better. A church potluck."

"Is this official police business?"

"Undercover . . . I'm undercover. You're part of the cover."

"Am I required to bring food?"

"Is that a problem?"

"No, of course not. Time and place?"

"I'll pick you up at six."

"You're lucky I like you."

24

SEVERAL ATTEMPTS AT knocking and ringing the doorbell went unanswered at Craig Schlepp's house. A quick peek in the garage verified an empty stall where the white pickup truck should be.

Peter pulled out his phone and punched in the number for the sheriff's office.

"Hey, Boss," answered Travis.

"Do you know what Craig Schlepp does for a living?"

"Some kind of financial guy. He has an office on the top floor of one of those old brick buildings on Main Street."

"Address?"

Travis flipped through an outdated business directory and rattled off an address.

"Thanks."

"Sure, Boss."

Peter found the building. Inside, he climbed refurbished and freshly polished stairs to the second floor. Professional offices lined a wide hallway, each proprietor declared in gilt lettering on frosted glass. A door marked 'Schlepp Investments' opened into a reception area, simple, yet stylish.

The young receptionist glanced at her appointment book and then back up at Peter. "Did you have an appointment? I don't show you in the book."

"No appointment, but I'd like to speak with Mr. Schlepp."

"He's not in today. Could I make an appointment for another day or is there something I could help you with?"

"Do you know where he is?"

"We don't give out private information."

"I'm not here as a client. This is a legal matter."

The receptionist hesitated. "Well, since it's you, Sheriff, he called in early this morning and said he wasn't feeling well. I canceled all his appointments."

"Did he say when he'd be back?"

"He canceled for the rest of the week."

Peter handed her a card. "If you hear from him, please have him call me."

Heading out, he passed a coat tree. A lone man's scarf emblazoned with a distinctive family crest stood out next to a woman's beige coat. "Does this belong to Mr. Schlepp?" asked Peter, lifting the scarf off the hook.

"Uh . . . yeah, he's always forgetting something."

"Tell you what, I'll take it over to him. Being sick and all, he might need a warm scarf."

She gave him an odd look. "Uh . . .okay. That's nice of you."

Outside the door, Peter pulled an evidence bag out of his duty vest and deposited the scarf. He hurried to his vehicle and punched in the number for the sheriff's office.

"Yeah, Boss," said Travis.

"Hey, Travis. I think Craig Schlepp is making a run for it. Put an APB out for him and his truck."

"Got it."

Peter started his vehicle and turned toward Tony Celares's house.

"Get your sniffer ready, Zack."

Peter drove to the Celareses' house, let Zack out of his kennel compartment and fastened the trailing harness and lead. He removed the scarf from the evidence bag and held it under Zack's nose, hoping Zack could separate Craig Schlepp's smell from the overpowering odor of old blood permeating the house. Zack sniffed, but he ignored the blood on the floor. Peter led him through the house, down the back hallway and out the door. Zack showed no interest.

"You're telling me Craig Schlepp hasn't been anywhere near this house?" asked Peter.

Zack nuzzled the vest pocket where he knew treats were kept.

THE RENTAL CABIN was an easy open for Angus, mainly because it hadn't been locked since Patty and Jerry were arrested. Keys to the black Honda lay conveniently in the middle of a breakfast nook table. Considering Patty's protective nature toward the car, Angus decided to search there first.

Several cardboard boxes filled the hatchback. Angus took out his camera and photographed everything in place before pulling a box out and setting it on the ground. He opened the crisscrossed flaps and stared in amazement. Superman flew across a perfect sky, emblazoned on a vintage school lunch box. The Beatles and Mickey Mouse danced to separate tunes on their own lunch box stages. Curious, Angus pulled out another box and opened the flaps. Once again, Superman stared back at him, this time encased in the clear front of a smaller black box.

Comic books?

Another box held a mixed assortment of jewelry stowed in clear plastic cases.

Before transferring the boxes into the cargo area of his patrol vehicle, Angus documented the contents. His instincts and the Giannettis' reputation told him these were stolen goods.

Returning to the Honda, he opened the doors to the middle seats and found the bubble wrapped paintings.

With more care than he used with the boxes, he transferred the paintings to the middle seats of his Ford Explorer.

Leaving the detailed investigation for Helen, Angus locked the car and headed toward the cabin. One level with an open floor plan, more because of size restraints than design, had the kitchen and dining to the left, living area to the right, and two doors in the rear leading to a bedroom and tiny bathroom. Well-used and mismatched couch and chairs in the living area and dishes in the cupboards spoke of a rental unit furnished with cheap castoffs. A brief walk-through showed nothing significant in the main area. Dishes in the kitchen sink and a Hollywood gossip magazine next to a half empty glass of wine on the coffee table were the main signs of human habitation. The bathroom also showed signs of short-term occupation. Travel-sized toiletries crowded the sink and shower shelves.

In the bedroom, things got more interesting. Bedside tables held sleep aids, anti-snoring nose strips, and paperback novels. Romance for Patty and westerns for Jerry . . . or the other way around. Who was Angus to judge?

Socks, underwear, T-shirts, and jeans filled the drawers of a second-hand dresser. Several church-worthy dresses hung in the closet next to men's button-down shirts. Behind the dresses and shirts stood two large suitcases. Angus pulled them out, searching side pockets and brushing his hand across the linings, feeling for hidden papers. Both were empty, but Angus took them out to his vehicle, leaving a closer inspection of the linings for later.

Angus locked the door, secured the keys for both the cabin and the Honda, and drove to the sheriff's office. Even with Travis's help, it would take the rest of the afternoon to log and secure three boxes of stolen goods and the pile of paintings.

HOUSES ON BOTH sides and across the street from Susan and Tony's showed little sign of activity with most families away at work and school. Peter unharnessed Zack, put him in his kennel with a treat, and walked to the house on the right side of the Celareses'. He rang the doorbell and waited a reasonable amount of time with no response before going to the house directly across the street. A flutter of the front window curtain told him there was someone home, proven when an elderly woman in a drooping housecoat answered the door as soon as Peter's finger left the buzzer.

"I've been watching you folks snoopin' around over there at the Celareses. What's going on anyway?" she asked.

"When's the last time you saw either Tony or Susan?"

She thought. "Oh, a few days ago, I suppose. Most mornings I hear Tony leaving for work. Susan doesn't have a regular schedule. If she's not gone somewhere, she stays in the house. My television programs start around dinner time so I don't pay attention in the evenings."

"Have you seen anything unusual going on?"

"With Tony and Susan? No, but I'm not the person to ask. You should talk to Herb Dorn on the other side." She pointed across the street. "He's the one who has to put up with her."

"With Susan?"

"Yeah. She's a piece of work."

Peter wrote down the woman's name and address, thanked her, and made his way back across the street.

Expecting an elderly man, Peter was surprised when a young man in his twenties answered the door before Peter had time to ring the bell.

"Herb Dorn?"

"Yeah. I know, I know. You were expecting my grandfather. My mom couldn't decide between Sage and Basil so she settled on Herb."

"You live here alone?"

"Yeah. For a coupla' years now. My parents moved south to a warmer climate and left me the house. I work from home if you're wondering. Software designer."

"How well do you know your neighbors?"

"The Celareses? Better than I'd like. Come on in and I'll tell you about it." He opened the door wider and stepped aside so Peter could pass.

Herb led Peter into a pleasant kitchen decorated with sunflowers and denim. "My mom's décor, if you're wondering," said Herb, he motioned for Peter to sit at a rustic wooden table. "Coffee?"

"Do you have tea?"

"Earl Grey?"

"Perfect."

"So, what's going on with the Celareses?" asked Herb while he prepared tea.

"When's the last time you saw them?" asked Peter.

"Hmmm. Not to sound like a nosy neighbor, but my work computer faces the front window so I see a lot of what's going on in the street." He brought steaming mugs of tea to the table.

"Isn't that a distraction?"

"You would think, but working from home can be isolating. Being able to see outside helps me feel connected to the world."

"So, that's why your neighbor sent me over here. She knows you watch the street."

Herb laughed. "Yeah, she called to let me know you were coming . . . hence the door opening as soon as you walked up."

"So, when was the last time you saw the Celareses?" Peter asked again.

"A few nights ago." He glanced at Peter. "It's not like I keep a record or anything. With Tony's parents murdered and all, I would expect things to be different, but there haven't been lights on in the house for days and I haven't seen any cars coming or going. Seems strange. When you and the dog and the other deputy started showing up, I knew something was going on."

"Do you remember anything specific about the last time you saw movement over there? Any vehicles or people besides Tony and Susan?"

"A few days ago, Tony came home from work. Susan's car left a little while later. I remember that specifically because I was here in the kitchen and saw her drive down the alley. That was strange. Susan never goes down the alley."

"Susan was driving?"

"I assume so, but couldn't swear to it. I saw the car go by. Who else?"

Two windows lit the bright kitchen. One above the sink looked out over a backyard and into the alley. The other faced a side yard and a tall wooden fence blocking the view of the Celareses' backyard.

"Not a friendly fence," said Peter. "Susan put that up?"

"No, me actually. My defense against her constant complaints. My grass was either too short or too tall. She found dandelions in her yard and it was all my fault. The complaints were never ending. I don't know how my parents put up with her for so many years. Now she complains about the fence, but it's within city codes so there's nothing she can do about it."

"I didn't know we had a city code about fences," said Peter.

Herb laughed. "We don't."

"What about Tony? Any issues with him?"

"Tony? No, he's a nice enough guy. I always wondered how he ended up with a cold fish like Susan."

⸻ ⬥ ⸻

SHARP KICKS WOKE Tony. Cold, thirsty, and in pain, he'd prayed to die in peace, but his abductor wasn't finished with him.

"Do you love your wife, Tony?" asked the voice.

Tony nodded, too dry to talk or cry.

"Do you want Susan to live?"

More nods.

"This is your last chance. You tell me where the loot is and you'll both live. Otherwise—"

"Please. Please no," whispered Tony. "What loot?"

"The gold, you moron. I want the gold."

"What gold?"

"Your parents' gold. Shame about them freezing to death, but they don't need that gold anymore."

Tony's body shuddered in silent sobs. "My parents don't have any gold."

A vicious laugh followed a final angry kick. "Lucky you. You get to die like your parents."

A muted click extinguished the soothing, life-giving warmth of the overhead heater. The door slammed, leaving Tony lying in silence and defeat as he felt the harsh cold of the cement seep into his body.

25

Built on the outskirts of Missoula, suspended over a serene lake, the steak house was the perfect location for a romantic anniversary dinner.

Clem pulled into the parking lot, shut off the ignition, and sat in her car listening to the engine tick as it cooled. Thick snowy white hair worn in loose waves and fashionable clothing gave her an air of confidence on the surface. Inside, she felt like a fraud. For the first seven decades of her life, she wore her hair pulled back in a ponytail. Dressing up meant putting on clean jeans. A fancy meal out took place at the local diner. Clem was a ranch kid and then a ranch wife because that's what was expected.

She flipped down the visor and studied herself in the vanity mirror. Mascara and cotton candy pink lipstick couldn't disguise the age in her eyes or the crinkles around her lips. Sure, she had a degree in forensics. That didn't make her an investigator. Longing to be taken seriously, Clem studied women detectives on television and dressed accordingly. Of course, the women on TV were decades younger and actually had badges, but that couldn't be helped. She took a deep breath, straightened her spine, and plastered a smile on her face.

⁕

SHE ARRIVED AFTER lunch and before the dinner rush, the visit carefully planned so the manager would be available for uninterrupted conversation. A bored hostess led Clem to the manager's office, showed her to a comfortable chair in front of his desk, and offered her a refreshment while she waited.

"A cup of coffee would be nice, black," said Clem. "Thank you."

Soon after, the manager hurried in carrying the promised cup of coffee. Tall and rangy from a lifetime in service, he seemed younger than Clem expected.

"Dale Ellis," he said as he set the cup in front of her and extended his hand.

"Thank you for taking the time to meet me," said Clem.

"I'm intrigued," he said, choosing a chair next to Clem, rather than behind his desk. "That murder still bothers me after all these years. Realistically, I was only a busboy. I didn't even remember seeing them here, but in the detective's eyes we were all suspect."

"What do you remember about that night?"

"Before the bodies were found? It was busy. The other busboy called in sick and I was on my own. There was a concert at the amphitheater on the other side of the lake. We give parking passes to our customers who have event tickets. It's good business. They come in for dinner and then walk around the lake for the concert."

"The Elliotts, the couple who were murdered, did they have concert tickets?"

"Yeah, that's where they were going when they got mugged."

"Can you show me?"

"Sure." Dale stood and grabbed a coat off a hook behind the door. "I'll show you where they were sitting first. It sounds silly, but it's been considered a bad luck table ever since. We rarely seat anyone there all these years later."

Dale led her to the outside deck. Although covered in snow and ice, Clem could imagine the young couple, Peter's parents, sitting on the deck on a warm summer evening. During the summer, fairy lights wrapped around deck railings and candles flickered at each table. Water, iced over now, lapping at the lakeshore. Chirping crickets and an occasional hoot owl would have added to the music of the night.

Dale showed Clem a small table shoved into a corner at the edge of the deck railing.

"Why do you keep the table? Why not take it out?"

"As a reminder. New employee training includes the murder story and a warning to watch out for any sign of danger to our customers. No one is allowed to walk the path without an escort. We have extra people on staff for concert nights."

Clem took pictures of the table and how it was placed in relation to the rest of the area.

"Were the other tables filled that evening?"

"Up until the bodies were found."

Clem recalled the murder file: *Everyone left in the restaurant that night, including diners, had been detained and questioned.*

"Show me where the bodies were found."

"If you walk straight out the back door and toward the lake," said Dale, "there's a fieldstone path that follows the lake around to the amphitheater." He pointed over the deck railing. "It's covered in snow so you can't see the path, but you can see the posts and solar lanterns that light the way."

A line of frosted black posts and lanterns peeked through the snow. Clem took pictures of them from the deck before Dale led her out the back door and to the path. Allowing the lanterns to guide them, they walked around a corner until they were hidden from the line of sight of the restaurant.

"It was right about here," said Dale. "As you can see, they were secluded."

Clem gazed across the lake. The sun was going down and darkness would soon fall, but it was a small lake and she could easily see to the opposite shore. "The police report says someone across the lake witnessed the mugging."

"That's true, another concert goer. He heard Mrs. Elliott scream and ran for help, but the Elliotts were shot and killed before anyone could do anything. All he saw was a man dressed in black with a black face covering."

"According to the report, the mugger ran into the woods."

Dale showed Clem a narrow opening in the woods next to the path. "There's a footpath through here that comes out at Reserve Street. The path also leads to the Clark's Fork River. Kids, fishermen, kayakers . . . you name it. There was no way to separate the mugger's footprints from everyone else who walked down the path."

"You know the case well."

He blushed. "It's been an obsession of mine, to the point I was a suspect for a while . . . you know, someone close to the case who is way too interested. Plus, all the busboys and wait staff were required to wear black so I was dressed like the suspect."

"But you were cleared?"

"Too many witnesses saw me in the restaurant before, during, and after. There was no way I had time to lurk in the path waiting for a victim, and then go back to work."

"Do you think the Elliotts were targeted?"

Dale thought for a moment. "Not specifically. A whole lot of people knew concert goers would have dinner at the restaurant and then take the path to the amphitheater. My opinion? The mugger wasn't a transient. He was someone local. Someone familiar enough with the woods and the path to know how to escape without a trace."

But Clem knew something Dale didn't, information in the police murder file not disclosed to the public.

26

Peter and Dixie arrived to find the church parking lot full and cars spilling into the surrounding field.

"I thought this was a church potluck," said Dixie, stepping carefully around rocks and over snowbanks.

"It is, but word gets around. They usually turn into community potlucks."

"So, nobody will be suspicious that we're here."

"Nope. The trick will be trying to figure out which people we need to question."

"How will we manage that?"

"Linda. She'll point us in the right direction."

The line of folks waiting to fill their plates wound around the perimeters of the church hall and out the door. Linda stood in the doorway waiting to take food offerings off the hands of new arrivals.

"Fried chicken?" she asked Dixie, pointing to her insulated casserole tote.

"Just like Mama used to make."

Peter watched as Dixie handed the tote over to Linda and took her place in line. "You're going to save some of that for me, aren't you?"

"There's so much good food here, Peter, by the time you're done sampling everything, you won't even be thinking about Dixie's chicken."

Dixie leaned over and whispered, "I brought an extra for you. It's under the seat of your truck."

Peter smiled, "Not sure I deserved that, but thanks."

Baptist women are professional potluckers, and the line moved fast. Plates piled high, Peter and Dixie scanned the room for empty seats. A bright red head of hair caught Peter's attention.

"Is that Angus?" he asked Dixie.

She looked in the direction where Peter pointed. "It sure is, and Travis and Helen are with him. There's extra chairs too."

Peter led her across the room. "Who's keeping law and order?" he asked as they sat.

Angus laughed. "Birdie and Debbie. We promised to bring them plates."

Peter wanted to ask how his search of the Giannetti property went, but it would have to wait. Too many interested ears were pointed their way. He'd already gone through the food line fending off questions about the murders of Frank and Alice Celares. Instead, they talked about upcoming Christmas events and visits to out-of-town family.

As usual, after-dinner evolved into social hour. Musicians tuned instruments and a variety of deserts were laid out on serving tables. Angus and Travis left with bulging aluminum foil wrapped plates. Peter, Dixie, and Helen split up to work the crowd in different corners of the room.

"Peter! Peter!" called a familiar voice. Nancy May rushed over dressed in red adorned with white snowflakes and a floppy hat to match.

"Hey, Nancy. You look fully recovered."

"Recovered? Oh . . . from the lights parade incident." She waved her hand in dismissal. "All in the line of duty."

She glanced around and pulled him aside. Leaning in close, she whispered, "Are you undercover?"

He whispered back, "You're not going to tell anyone, are you?"

"No. I'm going to help."

Oh boy.

"I see that expression, Peter, but I know which people to ask questions, besides Linda asked me to help."

"She did?"

"Sure. Linda knows who she can trust. She's over there helping your girlfriend, Dixie."

"She's not my girlfriend."

"Sure she is. You just don't know it yet. Now turn around and pretend we're talking about something besides stolen money."

"We are." An elbow jostled his arm.

"Oops, sorry, Sheriff. I'm wider than I think." Anne from the country club tried to scoot past carrying plates of goodies. "Nadine Ware is here with Mrs. Brady. They're both blind as bats. It's safer if someone else brings treats to them."

"Last potluck, Nadine was feeling around the table for a brownie," explained Nancy. "She knocked a whole bowl of cherry Jell-O on the floor. Mrs. Brady slipped in the puddle and bruised her tailbone."

"She never did get the stains out of that dress," said Anne.

"And they're still friends?" asked Peter.

"More like stale-mates. You should hear what Mrs. Brady did to Nadine . . ."

"So, Anne," said Peter, diverting the conversation, "have you seen Craig Schlepp today?"

She thought for a moment. "No, actually. He hasn't been to the country club, but he's probably at work. Is he in some sort of trouble?"

"Just need to chat with him."

Nancy grabbed Peter's arm and turned him toward the stage. "Peter, you must meet our new banjo player."

When they were well out of range of Anne, she said, "Those are the kind of nosy Nellies we need to avoid."

"Anne's a nosy Nellie?"

"The worst kind. Now, did you want to talk to the pro-Patty people or the pro-Alice people first?"

"Pro-Patty. The pro-Alice faction haven't changed their minds and Patty is the main suspect at this point."

"My thoughts exactly." She led him to a sheepish looking group huddled around a corner table.

"Hey, Nancy," mumbled a stocky middle-aged man in a faded plaid shirt.

"Hello, Stan. I see you've come to your senses."

Stan's lips pressed into a thin line and his face turned beet red. "I'm not the only one who got bamboozled by that woman."

"Was it the winking or giggling that had you thinking she was of fine character?"

"Now, that's not fair. There's plenty of women sitting at this table who thought a lot of Patty."

Nancy turned a critical eye on the women. "Peter and I—"

Peter cleared his throat.

"Well, Peter's investigating the missing offering and would like to ask all of you a few questions."

The group nodded in agreement.

Peter pulled an empty chair over from another table. "First, did any of you have Patty in your home and did you notice anything missing afterwards?"

"We talked about that," said Stan. "Most of us go out to lunch after church. We might have taken Patty and Jerry out, but we didn't take them home. Thinking back, she did ask a lot of questions. We were all flattered she was so interested. Now we can see she was digging for information on anything valuable she could steal."

"Fair enough," said Peter. "Next question. Are any of you responsible for the note that was nailed to the church door?"

He watched as everyone at the table looked at each other in confusion.

"What note?" asked Stan, the unofficial spokesman for the group.

"None of you know about the note?"

No's and headshakes passed around the table.

"Well, that answers that question. Do any of you have thoughts about the Celareses' murder, or information that would help us in our investigation?"

More no's and headshakes.

"Truth is," said Stan, "the money was all donations so it wasn't hurtin' our pocket books. We was mad when we thought Alice took it . . . all those years of trustin' her. We felt, well—"

"Betrayed," piped in a tall, bony woman.

"Patty twisted the story around to make it sound like she knew Alice did it," added another. "She has those big innocent lookin' eyes and is always so sweet. It was hard not to believe her."

"We feel real bad now," said Stan. "And Alice isn't around anymore to make it right."

The bony woman patted Stan's hand. "She knows now."

The group, in unison, looked toward heaven.

"I wish she could tell me who murdered her," said Peter. He stood and handed cards around the table. "If any of you thinks of anything else, please call me."

"Where to next?" asked Nancy.

"Let's gather up Dixie and Helen and see if they had any luck."

27

PULLING INTO THE Aspen grove at the end of Angela Brown's lane, Angus considered his options. He could sit for hours watching her driveway on the off chance she left the house, or he could knock on her door and ask her where she went the day of the murders. Angus chose the latter.

The pack of dogs heard his motor before he got to the house. They burst through the doggie door, yipping and howling. Angela stood at the door, a look of resignation on her face.

"Knock it off, you knuckleheads!" she yelled through the screen. Like a swarm of insects, the dogs turned in one movement and headed back to the house.

Angus hesitated.

"They won't bother you." Angela opened the door. "Come on in. I'll make you a fresh cup of coffee."

<hr>

SITTING AT THE table, sipping their coffee, Angela broke the awkward silence. "I've been expecting you back."

"You lied to me."

"I was hoping you wouldn't notice."

"I probably wouldn't have if it weren't for the fresh snow."

"Can I be charged for lying to the police?"

"Depends. You said you hadn't been anywhere for days. Tell me where you went after the snowfall and why you lied about it."

She fiddled with an ink pen, flipping it end to end and tapping nervously on the table. Angus waited.

"Pure pride. Pride and shame all rolled into one is why I lied."

She took a sip of coffee. "After Asher died, I started drinking." She looked at Angus. "I was never much of a drinker before that. But, I was . . . so broken . . . so alone. Oh, people tried. They brought me food and offered to help out around the place until I got back on my feet, but—"

Tears came and then dissolved. She took a napkin from a holder and wiped her eyes.

Angus waited.

"I was so angry. So angry. I wanted Frank Celares to die. One day Linda Elliott showed up," she glanced at Angus, "you know, the sheriff's sister-in-law."

Angus nodded.

"It was early in the morning and I was so drunk I could hardly walk. Probably still drunk from the day before. Days and nights, they all jumbled together. What did I care? People fed the animals and brought me food. What else did I need?"

She rubbed her forehead and stared into space, remembering. "Linda showed up that morning and I was drunk as usual. She stayed with me until I sobered up enough to drive me into town."

"What day was that?" asked Angus.

Surprised, she waved her hand in dismissal. "Oh, sometime last week, I think. Like I said, I was drunk all the time. The days all jumbled together. Linda brought me to the church where they were having an AA meeting."

"She's a good woman."

"A lifesaver for me. I probably would have drunk myself to death."

Angus waited.

She looked up and smiled. "That's where I went that day you saw the tracks in the snow. I was having a bad day so I went to see Linda. I was too ashamed to tell you about my drinking."

"I'll need to verify your story."

"I told her you would be asking."

28

"STILL NO DONUTS?" asked Peter, walking into the sheriff's office the next morning to find a solemn crew staring at an empty desk top.

"Nope. Company-wide recall. Tom's hoping for a delivery tomorrow," said Travis.

"Ta da," said Peter, bringing a white bakery box from behind his back. He set the box on Travis's desk and lifted the top. "Fresh baked cinnamon rolls from Dixie's."

"Wow! Thanks!" said Travis. He brought a stack of paper plates over from the cupboard, taking the top two off the stack and adding a cinnamon roll to each. "Is this a good enough breakfast for the prisoners?"

"They can hardly complain about Dixie's fresh baked cinnamon rolls," said Peter.

While Travis brought breakfast downstairs to the prisoners, the rest of the crew filled their own plates. Peter flipped a chunk of roll to Zack, and they settled in to discuss case updates.

"We didn't question the pro-Patty church folks separately at the potluck, but I'm not feeling a lot of murderous anger in that direction. Patty fed them a pretty believable story. If Alice were still alive, she'd be hearing quite a few humble apologies. Dixie got the same feeling," said Peter.

"Anyone fess up to the note nailed to the church door?" asked Angus.

"No. It doesn't fit either. They were all more disappointed in Alice than ready to kill her and, as Stan said, the money was all donations. It didn't hurt their finances. How'd you do, Helen?"

"Same. Didn't hear a lot of anger. Disappointment, disgust at the most. My thoughts are the missing church funds angle is a dead end."

"And the note on the door?"

"Still a mystery. Could it have been someone outside the church?"

"That would be my guess. What's new with you, Angus?"

"I talked to Angela Brown. She was visiting Linda Elliott that day."

"Why'd she lie about it?"

"Linda got her into AA. She didn't want to admit to a drinking problem. Anyway, I called and confirmed with Linda."

"Has anything come back on those APBs for Tony, Susan, or Craig?" asked Peter.

"Not a thing," said Travis. "But word around town is Tony has a cabin at Georgetown Lake."

"Do you think he would go there if he was running scared?" asked Helen. "Seems kind of obvious."

"Probably not, but if he's there we have one less missing person."

"Speaking of talk on the street, I haven't heard a peep out of Mavis or the mayor in days," said Peter. "Any gossip in that direction?"

"Lots of folks are mad about what happened over at the grocery store," said Travis. "There's talk of boycotting the paper and calling a special election to oust the mayor. Mavis and Kalinski are too busy trying to save face and put the blame on anyone else to be bothering us."

"Good. What do you have going on today, Helen?"

"I still need to do a thorough search of the Giannettis' car and house."

"Okay, you do that and you'll still be in town if anything comes up. Angus can check out the cabin at Georgetown."

Travis, back from the jail cells, opened a folder on his desk. "Cross-referencing the items found in the Giannetti car, most of them match a theft report. Until a year ago, all of their arrest records were limited to a small area of New Jersey."

"Matches the license plates and accents. Then what?" said Helen.

"They started on a cross-country crime spree, stealing enough along the way to fund their trip. Pennsylvania and then Ohio are clear, but that could mean they didn't get caught. We only know they were in those states from traffic stops. By the time they got to Indiana, they narrowed their target to churches. After a few months of Patty charming the congregation, they emptied the offering plate and made off with anything else they could get their hands on."

"Any chance of connecting the items we found with the victims?"

"They've been notified. The vintage lunch boxes belong to an elderly man in Indiana. He's been collecting them since he was a kid. Patty offered to organize his collection. By the time he realized they were gone, so were Patty and Jerry. The comic books came from a guy in Iowa. He's a dealer. The theft almost broke him."

"How did they manage to get ahold of those?"

"Patty offered to clean his shop. Gave him a sob story about needing extra money."

"And the jewelry?"

"Most of those are separate pieces reported by people across all those states, and South Dakota. As far as I can tell, when the Giannettis hit Montana, they came straight to Anderson."

"You think Anderson was their destination or just a coincidence?" asked Angus.

Travis shrugged. "No idea."

"If they stole the church funds and Nadine Ware's paintings, why did they stick around?" asked Helen. "Why didn't they get out of town before they were caught? Something kept them here."

"Another scam in process?"

"Let's bring Nadine in and see if she can ID those paintings. Then we'll have a chat with Patty and Jerry."

"Do you think she can see well enough to ID anything?" asked Helen.

"I'm not sure she even knows what paintings were there. Her husband did the collecting," said Peter. "I'll visit with her. She may have an inventory list."

Peter whistled to Zack and tossed his plate and crumbs in the trash on the way out the door.

29

WARMER DAYS AND melting snow took their toll on Porcupine Creek Road. Peter battled deep ruts on his way to see Nadine.

Ears ever on alert for a visitor, she stood waiting at the door when he drove up to the house.

"Who's there?" she called.

"Sheriff Elliott, Mrs. Ware," he let Zack out of his kennel compartment and met Nadine at the door.

"The sheriff again. That's twice in one week. My neighbors are gonna start gossiping."

"How many neighbors do you have, Mrs. Ware?"

"Well, none close enough to notice if I have visitors. Get on in here and bring your doggie."

She led Peter to the same plush armchair. The ancient corgi rose on stiff legs to greet Zack, then curled back up on his mat in front of the warm electric fire.

"Wait right here. I have a special treat. One of those neighbors came by with a peach pie yesterday. You don't often get peach pie in the winter."

After several minutes, Nadine came back with two giant pieces of pie and two doggie treats balanced on a tray. She set the tray on the table between the chairs and Peter tossed the doggie treats to Zack and his friend.

Settled in her chair, Nadine said, "My daughter worries about my eyesight. She thinks I should move into a retirement home, but I do fine here on my own."

"Does your daughter visit often?"

"No, never. She lives halfway across the country. She's busy with her kids and her work."

"Sure."

"Truth is, Sheriff, Sheila's always been a city girl . . . couldn't wait to grow up and move away from here. The last thing she wants to do is visit."

Peter cleared his throat. "I was wondering about your eyesight."

"Are you wanting to put me in a home, too?" asked Nadine, a tremor in her voice.

"Not at all. I'm wondering how well you can see." He gestured toward the wall. "These paintings, for instance, your husband's retirement investment. How long has it been since you've had a good look at them?"

Nadine glanced vaguely toward the walls. "Well, to tell you the truth, I didn't pay much attention to them when I could see. They aren't my cup of tea, but Marv said they weren't for lookin' at."

Peter considered possibilities. "How long since Marv passed on?"

"Two years in April."

"Have you had much company in the house since then?"

"Hmmm. Not so much since the funeral and all the family left. Patty coming along was a breath of fresh air, brought life back into this old house. Before that, the church folk would pull up and honk for me to come out."

Peter stood and took Nadine's hand. "I want to show you something."

Confused, she stood and allowed him to lead her to a wall. He brought her to a spot with an empty frame.

"What can you tell me about this painting?"

She stood close and peered with cloudy eyes, then reached up to touch the bare wall behind the empty frame.

"I . . . I don't understand. Where's the painting?" She felt her way along the wall from bare areas where paintings had once hung to additional empty frames. "Marv's paintings. They're all gone."

Peter felt Nadine sag and helped her back to her chair.

"I don't understand," she repeated.

"Nadine, Patty and Jerry Giannetti are in jail. We believe Patty stole your paintings."

"Jail? Patty? Why would she take my paintings?"

"She and Jerry have arrest warrants out from several states for theft. It's what they do, join a church, make friends, and steal from people."

"Oh, my."

"The good news is we think we have your paintings. We need you to come down to the sheriff's office and identify them. Do you have any documentation of ownership?"

"You have them?" Tears of relief welled up in her eyes.

"We think so. Documentation?"

"Oh, yes. Marv was very particular about that." Nadine pushed herself out of the chair. "But I'll need your eyes for this one."

Peter followed her into a small room off the living room, barely big enough to hold a secretary desk and a file cabinet.

"Look in the bottom drawer of that file cabinet under 'grocery lists'."

"Grocery lists?"

"It was Marv's little joke. He stored all our important papers in that file. He said it was the last place anyone would look."

Peter pulled open the bottom drawer and found the file. Inside he found everything from bank account information to social security numbers. Most importantly, he found a list of investment paintings including pictures.

Returning everything but the painting information to the file, Peter closed the drawer and said to Nadine,

"With this information and these pictures, I can ID the paintings for you."

"And you'll bring them back to me?"

"As soon as I can."

<hr>

WITH STEEP ROCKY cliffs threatening to drop car-eating boulders onto the road on one side and sheer drops on the other, Angus pitied the person required to traverse the twists and turns of the mountain pass between Anderson and Georgetown Lake on a regular basis. Winter added snow and ice, making the drive that much more treacherous.

Knowing of an ongoing argument between county and state over responsibility for plowing Georgetown roads, Angus was relieved to find the route to Craig Schlepp's cabin well-traveled and well maintained. The cabin sat on a hillside surrounded by trees that gave a sliver view of the lake. If Craig were looking for seclusion, this would be a good spot.

Angus opened his vehicle door and pulled on the snow boots he had stowed on the passenger side floorboard.

Unblemished snow packed the driveway to the cabin. There was no garage or any other place to hide a car. No smoke rose from the chimney. No light glowed in the windows. Angus waded through the snow to the cabin deck and knocked on the door, not expecting an answer. He peaked through windows into deserted rooms. Nothing.

A search around the cabin perimeter showed no footprints other than rabbits and deer. A wasted trip.

⬧⬧⬧

HELEN SEARCHED THE Giannettis' rental cabin first, but didn't find anything beyond what Angus had already documented. The Giannettis were people in transit with no intention of staying long term.

She searched the car, under the seats and in the console. Amongst the typical console debris—packs of gum, pens, and sunglasses—Helen found an envelope stuffed with a stash of cash. She smiled when she found several checks made out to Flint Creek Valley Baptist Church in another envelope. The church would get at least part of their money back. She photographed and documented her findings and moved on to the glove box.

On top of a pile of outdated registration slips, insurance cards, and road maps, lay a manilla envelope folded in half. Unclasped and opened, it revealed a pair of newspaper clippings, yellow and brittle with age, pasted on thick paper. One told a story of an airport heist and missing gold bars, the other a shootout between mafia thugs. Underneath, freshly printed from a computer, a news article told of a tragic bus accident in a small county in Montana.

30

ETER FOUND TRAVIS and Helen so engrossed in their investigation, they both jumped when he came into the office. Helen's pen flew out of her hand, just missing Zack's nose.

"We may have a connection between the Celareses and the Giannettis, but we haven't quite figured out what it is," said Helen.

"Really?" said Peter, surprised.

Helen showed him the newspaper articles she found in the Giannettis' glove box and summed them up, "Fifty some years ago, twenty gold bars were stolen from an airport in New York. Law enforcement suspected the mob was involved, but there were no arrests and the gold was never recovered."

"We researched the heist," said Travis. "Guess which mob family name came up first on the suspect list."

Peter shrugged. "No idea."

"The Giannettis."

"What?! No kidding? Those two are mobsters?"

"Possible relations. According to the article, the cargo handler on duty at the airport was connected to the family, too," said Travis.

"Not long after that, two cars were found on the outskirts of town," explained Helen. "Major gun action. Seven bodies. As far as the anyone could tell, everyone involved died of their wounds."

"This from the second article?" asked Peter.

"Yep. Two mob families involved, the Giannettis and the Baglionis."

"Was this related to the gold heist?" asked Peter.

"If it was, the gold was long gone before the cops showed up."

Peter studied the thick paper the two articles were pasted on. One long edge was torn away from its origins. "Looks like they ripped this out of a scrapbook."

"That's what I thought," said Helen. She held up the newly printed sheet. "This is a copy of an article about Frank Celares's bus accident."

"This was with the other two?"

"Same envelope. Guess where I found them."

Peter shrugged again.

"In the Giannettis' glove box."

"I'm not surprised the Giannettis have criminal connections, but how is the Celares bus accident involved?"

"That's what we're trying to figure out."

Helen showed Peter the cash and checks she found in the Giannettis' car. "With this, we have Patty for the church theft."

"That's a relief." Peter took out the list of investment paintings he got from Nadine. "Let's compare these to the ones we found. Nadine said there should be labels on the backs of the paintings to match the list. If they match, it's time to talk to the Giannettis."

Travis and Helen followed Peter into his office where he had the paintings secured in a locked closet. One by one, they compared the list to the label on the back of the painting. Every painting was accounted for.

"Lucky for Nadine, they didn't have a chance to unload these," said Helen.

"Yeah, lucky," said Peter. "I'll give her a call and let her know they're safe."

"Patty stole paintings from Nadine and money from the church. I wonder what she stole . . . or tried to steal from Alice and Frank Celares," said Travis.

"Good question. Time to talk to Patty."

⚬⚬⚬

HAIR IN DISARRAY, clothing rumpled, hands in cuffs, Patty Giannetti smiled a coy smile, giggled and attempted charm. "I didn't realize we had such a handsome sheriff in town."

Sitting in the corner as a witness, Helen rolled her eyes.

Ignoring the flirt, Peter began, "Priscilla Giannetti—"

"Oh . . ." she said, realizing the jig was up on her alias. "Please call me Patty."

"Priscilla Giannetti, you are being charged with theft of property—"

"What? What are you talking about?"

"Valuable paintings were stolen from the home of Nadine Ware. Funds in the form of cash and checks were stolen from the Baptist church. All of this was found in your vehicle."

"You broke into my car?!"

"No, we had the keys and a warrant."

The coy smile again. "This is all a silly misunderstanding. Nadine gave me those paintings as payment for helping her around the house. The church asked me to deposit that money in the bank."

"You are being charged with assault and the theft of property," continued Peter before reciting the Miranda warning, "Do you wish to have a lawyer present for questioning?"

"I see no reason for a lawyer. I've done nothing wrong. As soon as I chat with Nadine and Pastor Paul, we'll get this all straightened out."

Peter pushed a Waiver of Rights form across his desk. "Then you won't mind signing this." He handed her a pen. "Legal name please."

Patty lifted her cuffed hands onto the desk and signed the form. "There. Can I go now?"

"It's out of my hands. A judge has to make that decision."

An expression of fear crossed Patty's face before she rallied. "A judge? Why so serious? I'm sure we can work something out."

"Tell me, you know Frank and Alice Celares?"

"From church."

"Did you have other contact with the Celareses? Were you ever in their home?"

"I helped Alice out around the house after she slipped and broke her wrist. Poor dear."

"Did Alice compensate you for your 'help' around the house?"

"Uh, well, no. I helped Alice out of the goodness of my heart."

I doubt it, thought Peter.

"After you stole the special offering from the church and blamed Alice, did you continue 'helping' her around the house?"

"Now that's not fair, Sheriff, you have no proof—"

"Actually, yes, we do. When's the last time you were at the Celareses' house?"

"Uh . . . I don't know. You can't expect me to remember every little date."

"Was is before or after they were murdered?"

"What? You can't believe I had anything to do with that!"

"What brought you to Anderson?"

"What brought us here?"

"Yeah, why did you decide to move from New Jersey to Anderson, Montana?"

"We were tired of the city. Lots of people move to the country."

"Did you know Frank and Alice Celares before you came to town?"

"No."

Peter slid a copy of the bus accident new article across his desk. "Then why did you have this in your car?"

Patty glanced at the article and shrugged. "We heard about the accident. Someone gave me a copy of the article."

"Who?"

"Who, what?"

"Who gave you a copy of the article?"

Patty shrugged. "I don't remember. Someone from church."

Peter slid copies of the airport heist and mob shootout articles across his desk, "And these? What can you tell me about these?"

Patty eyes widened when she glanced at the copies. She pushed them back at Peter. "I don't know anything about those."

"They were in your car."

"Something Jerry was doing. They have nothing to do with me." Her mouth went into a pout. "This is boring. I have nothing else to say."

HELEN RETURNED PATTY to her cell and led a smug Jerry into Peter's office.

"You've got nothing on me and you know it," said Jerry as he flopped into the chair in front of Peter's desk. "In fact, I'm going to sue this department for assault."

"You are being charged with theft and threatening a police officer."

"Theft? Threats? Trumped up charges."

Peter recited the Miranda warning. "Do you understand these rights?"

"Yeah, yeah."

"Would you like a lawyer present before we began questioning?"

"Like I said, you got nothin' on me."

Peter slid a Waiver of Rights form and a pen across his desk. "Then you won't mind signing this."

Jerry read the form carefully before lifting his cuffed hands to the desk. He picked up the pen and scribbled an illegible scrawl across the paper. "Ask your questions so I can get out of here."

Peter slid copies of the airport heist and mob shootout articles across his desk. "What can you tell me about these?" He watched Jerry's face as he realized what he was looking at.

"Where'd you get these?" asked Jerry, anger bubbling to the surface.

"Out of your car."

"What were you doing in my car!" Jerry stood and tried to reach over the desk.

Helen yelled, "Sit down!" and pushed the button on her taser so Jerry could hear it crackle.

Giving Helen a death glare, Jerry dropped into the chair. "I had nothin' to do with that gold heist."

"Judging from the date on these articles," said Peter. "I'd say this was before your time. Your dad?"

"Yeah, well, he's dead so you can't get him on it either."

"He die in the shootout?"

"Yeah." An out of character sadness passed over Jerry's face.

"What happened to the gold?"

"Aahhh. I get it. You want a cut of the gold."

"Not a bit." Peter slid the copy of the bus accident news article across to Jerry. "I want to know what the gold heist and the shootout have to do with Frank and Alice Celares."

Jerry sat in silence for a moment. "Could I have something to drink?"

"Water? Pop?" asked Helen.

"Pop?"

"Soda," explained Helen.

"Yeah, I'll have a soda. Diet."

The room stayed silent while they waited for Helen to return. She handed him the pop can, but taking a drink was awkward.

"Can I have the cuffs off?"

Peter hesitated.

"I'm not going to do anything with her standing there holding that zap gun."

Peter nodded and Helen released the cuffs.

"What's in it for me?" asked Jerry. "If I tell you about the gold."

"We have witnesses that Patty stole the paintings and the money from the church. You had nothing to do with it."

"That's what I said."

"You tell us about the gold and how it connects to Frank and Alice and we'll forget about you threatening to punch the sheriff. The theft charges stay with Patty."

Jerry sipped his pop, cleared his throat and began.

31

"**I** WAS A KID when Pops died," said Jerry. "Life wasn't so good for Mom after that, with four kids and no income. There's no pension plan in the mob for widows and orphans. Mom moved us from New York to New Jersey to live with her parents."

"Tell me about the airport heist and the shootout that killed your dad?"

"Mom didn't talk about it . . . told us our father died in a car accident. We were too young to know better. I didn't know anything about his connection to the mob or the airport heist until after she died and I found those articles in a scrapbook."

"Must have been a shock."

"At first, but then other things started to make sense . . . the friend of Pops who sent us wads of cash, Mom always nervous and looking over her shoulder. I guess she expected someone to come looking at her for the gold."

"Do your siblings know?"

"Naw, two brothers and a sister. Good jobs. Happy kids. Not troublemakers like me. Mom always said I was the one who took after Pops. Now I know what she meant."

"So, your mom's gone, you find out about your dad and the heist, and start thinking about gold."

"I searched the rest of Mom's house hoping to find the gold, or at least a treasure map. I should have known if she had the gold we would have been living better and someone would have come after it a long time ago."

"Find anything else in your search?"

"My dad's friend, I only knew him as Uncle Paulie. I found his name and address in Mom's stuff. Paul Giannetti, a legitimate uncle. He still lives in the old neighborhood."

"You went to find him to get answers about your dad?"

"Yeah. Mom told us Pops was an insurance salesman," he laughed. "He sold insurance all right. Pay up or you die insurance."

"Did your Uncle Paulie know anything about the heist?"

"Pops and his crew planned the heist and pulled it off. Someone couldn't keep their mouth shut and another crime family, the Baglionis, heard all the details. They waited on the route from the airport and tried to take the gold.

Mobsters don't go down easy. When the shooting was over and they got the bodies sorted out, things didn't add up."

"How so?"

"Two cars, seven bodies. The cops didn't know any different, but the family did. Pop's driver was missing."

"According to the article, the gold was gone too."

"Twenty bars. Too much gold for someone to carry away. The first thing the family did was track down Pop's driver. Turns out he was in the hospital with a solid alibi. Emergency appendectomy. Pops had to find a fill-in driver for the heist."

"Wouldn't he pull in an associate? Someone close to the family?"

"Sure, but the heist was going down and Pops needed a driver fast. Anybody who knew who the new driver was died in the shootout."

"None of the other guys would have driven in a pinch?"

"Naw, they had their own assignments. Uncle Paulie said ranks are taken very seriously in the family. It would have been an insult to expect someone besides a driver to drive."

"If your dad pulled in another associate to drive, would that person have time to plan a double cross?"

"Doubtful, especially back in those days. No cell phones. Pops wouldn't have let a driver know what was going on anyway. If drivers hear anything, they keep their mouths shut or . . ." He made a slicing motion across his throat. "After the heist, everyone wanted the gold. The key was

the driver. It's hard to keep much private in the neighborhood . . . like a small town, you know."

Peter nodded. He did know.

"Uncle Paulie heard of a young guy around the neighborhood, not part of the family. The guy and his wife
disappeared the same night as the heist. Left his house
with everything in it. Didn't even tell his parents where he
was going. If the guy was by himself, people would have
chalked it up to him getting whacked by the mob, but
with his wife missing too and them newly married . . ."

"Did the guy have a name?"

"Yeah, Frankie Celares. Married to Alice Celares. No
kids, but one on the way."

"Frank and Alice Celares. They didn't even change
their names."

"It was harder to track people back then. They probably
drove until their cash and the road ran out and didn't
think anyone would ever look for them in a small town
in Montana."

"But, you found them."

"I had what nobody had back then, names and the
Internet. Every now and then I would search their names.
They kept a low profile until that bus accident."

"How did you know it was the same people or that
they still had the gold?"

"I didn't, but in my thinking, that gold was stolen
from Pops. He's dead so it's rightfully mine. It was worth
driving a couple thousand miles to find out."

"Tell me about when you got to town."

"We rented that cabin and started asking around. You've probably figured out Patty does this thing where she gets involved in a local church, marks a couple chumps for a take and then makes off with cash from the plate."

"This time she found the church Frank and Alice attended."

"Yeah. She blew it when she ran off with that cash though. I told her it was too soon, but she said everyone would blame Alice."

"Did you go to Frank and Alice's house?"

"No, but Patty did."

"You expect me to believe you came all the way here to find Frank and Alice and didn't go to their house?"

Back with the smug look. "You're trying to pin that murder on me and it won't happen. Talk to Patty. She was up there."

"Put him back in his cell, Helen."

"What?! You said I could go if I talked."

"You're a murder suspect. We find out it was someone else, we'll talk."

32

"WE'VE GOT CRAIG Schlepp," said Travis, poking his head into Peter's office.

"Great! Where is he?"

"In a rundown motel outside of Missoula. A deputy stopped there on a domestic complaint and recognized Craig's truck from the APB."

———

TWENTY SOME MILES shy of Missoula, following directions given by the Missoula County deputy, Angus took the appropriate exit and turned onto a frontage road.

Eventually he came to an abandoned roadside café, windows boarded up and a faded realtor's sign attached to the door. On the far side of the lot stood a deserted gas station, pumps long ago removed. The sign from the same realtor hung in the window. A hand-painted sign attached to the café announced 'motel' with an arrow pointing between the buildings. Angus drove through and found a two-story motor lodge standing at the rear of the lot. If not for the spastic vacancy sign flashing in the office window, Angus would have pegged the motel as abandoned. Overgrown weeds split parking lot asphalt. Paint peeled away from sagging trim. Several broken and plywood covered windows were scattered among twenty rooms, ten above, ten below.

A Missoula County deputy stood next to a patrol vehicle in front of room three on the ground floor.

Angus pulled up next to him and got out. "You have him in custody?"

"In the car. He's a little owly. I didn't want to leave him in the room by himself."

Angus walked around the other vehicle as the deputy opened the rear door.

Craig Schlepp, wide-eyed, looked out from inside. "Am I under arrest?"

"Not yet," said Angus. "But we have a lot of questions." He motioned Craig out of the car. "This your room?" he asked, pointing to room three.

"Yeah."

"Would you be willing to sit with me and answer a few questions?" asked Angus.

"I didn't do anything wrong."

"This is your chance to tell your side of the story."

"Did you talk to Susan?"

"Susan is missing. We were hoping you could shed light on that."

Craig stepped out of the vehicle and reached into his pocket for his room key. "I don't know where Susan is, but I'll tell you what I do know."

Angus waved a thanks to the Missoula deputy and followed Craig into a shabby room well past its prime. Decades of sweat, cigarette smoke, and lackadaisical cleaning left an unpleasant odor in the air.

"Tell you what," said Angus. "There's a café off the next exit. They have a quiet back room they'd let us use. I'll buy you lunch."

"I'm not under arrest?"

"Nope. You can drive away right now if you want, but I hope you don't."

Craig nodded. "I shouldn't have run. After the murders, and then Susan disappeared . . . I got scared."

Angus opened the front passenger door of his patrol vehicle, motioned Craig in, and made his way to the café.

Angus showed a waitress his badge. "We have police business to discuss. Could we eat in the back room?"

"You're in luck," she said, with a sunny smile. "Our noon Rotary club meeting canceled." She led them through the busy café and into a narrow room with a long table taking up most of the center. Angus and Craig chose seats at the far end of the room. The waitress offered menus, but they both chose the fish and chips special.

"Oh good, we made that special for Rotary and were going to have a ton of leftovers."

To avoid being overheard and potential gossip spreading to Anderson, Angus waited until they were served to begin his questioning. "Do you mind if I record this?" he asked as he set down a small recorder.

"All right with me. The only thing I did wrong was not going to the sheriff in the first place. Where do you want me to start?"

"How about the beginning."

"Okay. Good. You know Susan Celares?"

"Not really."

"She's a member of the country club . . . a very active member. I'm the chairman of the board, but you probably already know that."

Angus nodded.

"Susan . . . well, she's a wannabee."

"A wannabee?"

"A wannabee somewhere else. A wannabee someone important. She wants to be a jetsetter, but she's stuck in this little town in Montana living a middle-class life."

Angus let him talk.

"Susan's the head of every committee and sprinkles glitter whenever she can. The Christmas gala is her big event of the year. She gets to dress up in a fancy gown and pretend she's not in a rundown building that's seen better days."

"How does that go over with the rest of the club?"

"Mostly, they're happy to let her do the bulk of the work, but . . ."

"But, there's another side."

"Yeah. Susan isn't just a wannabee, she's a 'thinks-she-is' as in she thinks she's better than most anyone else in the club . . . or in town for that matter."

"Has she made enemies?"

"You could say that. People don't appreciate being talked down to."

"Could you name anyone in particular?"

"I could give you a list of club members. Take your choice."

"There's been talk that you and she had a special relationship."

"Yeah, the other deputy mentioned that. I was definitely NOT having an affair with Susan Celares."

"So, what was going on?"

Craig took a few moments to chew a chip. "I'm also a financial adviser. That's what I do for a living. I don't usually recommend investing in gold, but occasionally I have a client who wants to go in that direction, so I keep abreast of current trends and help them buy and sell." He glanced at Angus. "I know real gold when I see it and know when someone brings me counterfeit."

Angus nodded in understanding. Years of watching his mother buy and sell antiques gave him the eye of a dealer himself.

"Susan called me a couple months ago and asked me to meet her at the club. After hours. Alone."

"Was that unusual?"

"Not the meeting. We met often when she was planning an event. After hours and alone was different. She was waiting for me in the parking lot. When we got to my office, she locked the door and pulled the shades. I thought she'd lost her mind."

"She brought you gold," guessed Angus.

"A bag of gold coins. Dumped them out in the middle of my desk."

"Counterfeit?"

"No, but not something she bought from a dealer."

"How so?"

"They were like something out of the old west, rustic. Imagine a grubby old miner panning for gold all day, melting it down at night, and pouring it into molds. That's a simplified version of the process, but you get my drift. These coins were crude. Homemade."

"You're positive it was real gold?"

"No doubt. Weight, color. It passed all the tests."

"Did she say where the coins came from?"

"She was vague at first. I got the feeling something wasn't on the up and up. She wanted me to help her sell them. I told her no."

"How'd she take that?"

"Not well. She changed her story and said she got them from family, but they wanted to keep it quiet."

"I told her I would think about it, but every time I saw her at the club, she pressured me to move forward. She kept offering me a higher percentage of the proceeds."

"How much money are we talking about?"

"Gold is a commodity. Prices can change daily. Rough coins would go for less than professionally poured, but they struck me as fairly pure in spite of an amateur molding job." He shrugged. "The coins weighed in at a little under three pounds. They could bring in as much as Tony Celares makes in a year. I've heard rumors that Susan spends more than he makes and things were getting dicey financially. That gold would plug the leak for a while."

"What brought you to the point of running?"

"First, Tony's parents were murdered. Susan was acting more squirrelly than ever, begging me to keep quiet about the gold. I confronted her, and she admitted the coins came from Tony's parents."

"Did she steal them?"

"Took them from a thief and then stole them herself."

"How does that work?"

"Susan said Alice slipped and broke her wrist. There was a woman from the church at the house supposedly helping out while Alice healed."

"Patty Giannetti."

"Yeah, that sounds right. Anyway, Susan said she didn't trust this Patty woman and would drive up there now and then to check on things. One day she saw the barn door open, went in, and found Patty snooping through old trunks and stuff. Patty didn't notice Susan watching and all of a sudden started whooping and hollering and dancing around. She'd found that bag of gold coins. Susan stepped in, took the coins, and told Patty to leave and never come back."

"Did Susan tell Alice and Frank about the coins?"

"I don't think so. That was one of the vague areas."

"Then Frank and Alice were murdered," prompted Angus.

"Yeah, When the other deputy, Miss Bradshaw, came and told me Susan and Tony were missing, I panicked and ran."

"Do you know where the gold is?"

"No. Susan took it that first day when she left."

Angus thought for a moment, excused himself, and went outside to call Peter. He relayed the highlights of his conversation with Craig.

"He sounds legitimate," said Angus.

"Yeah," said Peter, "but everyone lies."

"Where should we go from here?"

"I'll get a search warrant for his house. In the meantime, search his car and motel room. If he's as innocent as he says, he shouldn't have a problem with that. Look for anything that would connect him to the gold and a murder."

"If I don't find anything to arrest him on?"

"Tell him to come back to town and we'll have Birdie watch his house tonight. While she's 'protecting' him, we can be watching so he doesn't run off again."

33

"Did you find anything in Craig's car?" asked Peter when Angus got back to town.

"Not a thing. His car and motel room were both neat as a pin. I have a feeling if there's a receipt for gold, it's stored neatly in a file in his house."

"No answers and we have nothing to charge him with. Judge Knowles issued a search warrant for his house, but he could be home shredding the evidence as we speak."

"He could be lying about turning Susan down, and he's a bit too insistent about his dislike for her," said Helen. "Scenario: he and Susan knocked Tony over the head, stole the gold and disposed of Tony's body."

"Or he murdered Susan someplace else and dumped her body," said Angus. "Zack didn't find a trace of Craig at the Celareses' house."

"We only have Craig's word about Susan taking the gold from Patty," said Helen. "Susan could have been the one snooping around in the barn . . . maybe she's been looting that barn of treasures for years, but didn't know about the gold. Patty finds out Susan is Frank and Alice's daughter-in-law and tells her about the heist. Patty wants to go in together to find the gold. Susan turns her down and goes after it for herself. Susan had no reason to go in with Patty."

"But why make up the story about Patty?" asked Angus.

"She's a snob. She doesn't want Craig to know she's been pilfering from her in-laws. She tries to deflect on Patty. Also, it points a finger at Patty for the murders."

"Making Susan the suspect. She finds out about the gold and discovers the coins, but wants more. She ties Frank and Alice to chairs and threatens them, gets nothing out of them and leaves them to die."

"Patty could have done the same thing without approaching Susan," said Peter. "Maybe Susan did walk in and catch her in the act."

"Wouldn't she report it, though?" said Angus.

"Not if she wants to keep the gold secret, besides those coins can't be all that's left of twenty gold bars. Whoever found the coins is probably still looking for the rest."

"Why wouldn't Susan confront Tony about the treasure? If he knew about it, wouldn't he have told his wife?"

"Maybe not. She would have spent it years ago on a fancier house, cars, and clothes," said Helen.

"Whoever the murderer or murderers are, it's harder to hide a body in the winter when the ground's frozen and everything's covered in snow. We may find Tony and Susan sharing the remnants of a snowbank after spring thaw," said Angus.

"Who are we missing?" asked Peter. "Who's the wildcard?"

Travis studied his fingernails, Angus stared out the window, and Helen picked crumbs out of the donut box. Zack groaned and turned over on his bed.

"Hey," said Angus. "I think we should go up to Frank and Alice's house and search that barn."

"Good thought," said Peter. "You and Helen can both go, but first bring Patty back up. I want to compare her story to Susan's."

***

"TELL ME ABOUT your time at Frank and Alice's house," said Peter when he had Patty in his office.

"I told you; I helped her out with stuff after she broke her wrist."

"What kind of stuff?"

"Filing paperwork and stuff."

"It seems to me someone with a broken wrist would need help around the house. Dishes, vacuuming, cooking . . ."

"Oh, I don't do housework."

"So, like at Nadine's, you didn't actually help. Instead, you helped yourself to her treasures. What kind of treasures did you find at Alice's house?"

Patty crossed her arms and went into pout mode.

"Did you see anyone besides Frank and Alice while you were there? Neighbors come to visit? Family?"

"No."

"Nobody? Not even their son and daughter-in-law? Tony? Susan?"

"Whatever that snotty witch said, she's lying."

"So, you did see Susan at Frank and Alice's house?"

"Yeah. I forgot until you mentioned it."

"Tell me about it, you seeing her there."

"Nothing to tell."

"Where were you when you saw her? In the house? Outside? In the barn?"

"I don't do barns."

"So, you saw Susan in the house?"

"Yeah, sure."

"What did you and Susan talk about?"

"Nothing. She was rude to me and I took off. I don't need to take that from anyone."

"Were you looking for those gold bars from the heist way back in the day."

"I told you, that's Jerry's thing. I don't know anything about any gold."

"Did you tie Frank and Alice up and threaten them?"

She crossed her arms in a pout. "I know nothing about that. I'm done talking."

"Take her back to her cell, Angus."

34

"TOM WAS RIGHT about all the cool stuff," said Helen as she and Angus stood in the Celareses' barn entrance and stared in awe at a two-horse buggy parked along one wall. Behind it stood a horse-drawn sleigh.

Rows of saddles, bridles, and harnesses hung on the wall behind them along with several sets of chaps and an occasional cowboy hat. An assortment of dusty tools hung in another section.

"Were they collectors?" asked Helen.

"I don't think so. This looks like stuff that was used on the ranch a hundred years ago, before the Celareses bought the place."

"I can't believe they didn't have it locked up. Okay, focus. We're looking for treasure." She glanced around. "Besides all this. Where would we find gold?"

Angus shrugged. "I don't know. You start on that side and I'll start over here and we'll work our way to the back."

"Sounds good."

Mice skittered and old wood creaked as Angus and Helen searched, hoping they knew the treasure when they saw it. Moving about in the old barn stirred the dust and Angus went into a sneezing fit.

"You okay?" called Helen.

"Yeah, dust tickling my nose."

Helen found a feed room. Hoping for a cache of gold, she lifted the lids of the feed bins and instead found an abundance of mouse droppings, the grain long ago eaten away by rodents. Thoughts of hantavirus crossed her mind as she breathed in the stale air.

Back in the main room, Helen studied the floor. Rough wooden planks had softened through years of use, the cracks hard-packed with dirt and hay debris. Any lifting of planks to retrieve gold would be noticeable and Helen could see no signs of recent disturbance.

"Hey, Helen," called Angus from another room. "Come look at this."

Helen hurried to the rear of the barn, following Angus's voice. She found him next to a sturdy metal stand holding a wide bowl.

"What's this?" asked Helen.

"A portable blacksmith forge. A lot of ranches had them. They could be moved to wherever equipment needed fixing or horses needed shoeing. We have one at the ranch at home."

Born and raised on a century old cattle ranch over the mountain in Rumsey, Angus knew both the old and new ways of ranching.

Thick layers of gray ash filled the belly of the forge bowl.

"Coal ash," explained Angus. "Coal works best for forging because it burns longer and hotter than wood."

"How does the forge work?"

"This lever runs the bellows that blow air into the fire from underneath." Angus pumped the lever to demonstrate. He knelt and reached under the stand. "Down here there's a hopper to collect ash." He popped out a metal can and dumped a pile of ash in a nearby waste can. "The forge is simple. The skill comes in heating and working the metal."

Next to the forge sat a thick bench of wood holding a heavy block of metal, a flat rectangle on one end and a metal horn on the other. Several tools hung from the work bench.

"Here's the anvil and hammer," said Angus, "and a chisel and tongs."

Impressed, Helen asked, "Do you know how to blacksmith?"

"Not really. My grandpa did most of the blacksmithing on the ranch in his day. I watched him and he showed me a few things."

Angus walked to the outer wall of the room. "Look at this." He unhooked a latch and slid the wall to the side, turning the room into an open-air workshop. "Besides the risk of an open fire in the barn, breathing in the fumes from burning coal isn't a good idea either. They set this up to be an outdoor forge when they needed it."

"Cool!"

They both stood at the edge of the barn floor, breathing in fresh cold air.

"Look there," said Angus pointing to a pile of black chunks partially covered with snow. "Coal."

They stepped back. Angus slid the wall closed and fastened the latch. He walked back to the forge.

"Here's the interesting part of this setup," said Angus. "At first, I thought the forge was left over from when this was a working ranch . . . long before the Celareses bought the place, what . . . forty or fifty years ago? It should be rusted and unusable." He demonstrated the bellows again. "The gears are freshly oiled. The chain and belt are all newer than a century or even fifty years ago. Someone's been using this forge."

"But the Celareses weren't ranchers. They didn't even have horses. What would they be using it for?"

"Not blacksmithing. Look at this." Angus motioned for Helen to follow him to a cabinet at the edge of the room.

He pulled a pair of nitrile gloves out of his duty vest and opened the cabinet doors. Inside had the air of a medieval lab with heavy gloves, goggles, tongs, and a variety of odd shaped pots. Wool overalls and aprons hung from inside hooks.

"What is all this?" asked Helen.

"Graphite crucibles and molds. My guess? Jerry's story about the gold heist is true. Frank and Alice came to Montana with nothing but a trunk full of gold bars. Those bars weren't the little one-ounce size you would buy as an investor. They were the four hundred troy ounce bars that banks and governments keep hidden away in vaults. Trying to sell one would have raised eyebrows no matter where they went, because identifying marks would link the gold bars to the heist. Melting them down erased any proof of where they came from."

Helen stared at Angus, mouth open. "How do you know all this stuff?"

Angus smiled. "Grandpa used to pan for gold. All small-time stuff compared to this, but he saved his picker nuggets and flakes until he had enough to make it worthwhile to smelt and mold."

"Smelt is different than melt?"

"Gold . . . straight out of the ground, or creek if you're panning, is bound to rock and sediment and . . . well, everything else you find in the ground. The goal is to separate the gold and get it as close to pure as possible. That's smelting. Crushing and then melting burns off most of the impurities, but there's other metals attached to the gold. They have to be removed chemically using cyanide and mercury. When you hear about contamination left over from the old gold mines, that's the cyanide and mercury left over from smelting."

"Were Frank and Alice smelting?"

"Nope. No need. They had pure gold. All they had to do was melt it and pour it into molds."

"And they could do that with this old forge?'"

"Easy. Burning coal, this forge can reach a temperature of thirty-five hundred degrees Fahrenheit. The melting point of gold is much lower than that . . . just under two thousand degrees."

Helen pulled on a pair of gloves and picked up a stack of the small molds. "Circles. These are used to make the rough coins Craig Schlepp talked about."

"Yep." Angus picked up a plate mold of several small rectangles. "And small bars."

"What's this?" asked Helen, setting down the coin molds and picking up two larger forms.

She handed one to Angus and they both studied the shape.

"It's two sides of a guy holding a ball," said Angus.

"Oh," said Helen. "Oh . . . oh. We need to go to the house. Bring the mold."

Jogging toward the front of the barn, she yelled over her shoulder. "Do you have a key?"

"Yeah. I got it from Peter before we headed up."

INSIDE THE HOUSE, Helen went through the kitchen and thumped up the staircase, Angus at her heels. At the top, she bent over, gasping for breath.

"You okay?" asked Angus.

"Yeah. I really need to lose weight."

She stood, took a deep breath and walked down the hallway to the rear bedroom. Pointing toward the trophies lining the shelf along the wall, she said, "Can you reach those?"

Angus stretched and grabbed on to a trophy with one hand, then almost dropped it. "Wow! That's heavy."

He brought the trophy down with both hands. Helen held out her half of the mold. Minus the wooden base, the trophy fit perfectly into the mold.

"They were making molds of Tony's trophies and hiding the gold in plain sight," said Helen.

"Do you think Tony noticed?"

"I doubt it. Do you ever take old school trophies down from the shelf and look at them?"

"Uh . . . no."

"Exactly."

"Ingenious," said Angus staring at the row of trophies in awe. "Do you think they're all gold?"

"They do look a lot shinier than your average dusty trophy. And no tarnish." She counted seven bowling trophies. "A bar of gold per trophy?"

"Sounds right. How many were in the heist?"

"Twenty."

"Bowling trophies account for seven." He reached up and took down a little league trophy, dusty and tarnished. "Nope. This is the real thing."

"Some of the bars would have been melted down and molded to sell through the years. It paid for this place and Tony's fancy college degree back east."

"I don't think we should leave the trophies here. Someone else might find the molds and have the same epiphany."

Looking around the room, Helen saw the empty plastic bins that used to hold building blocks. "These should work."

Bins loaded, Helen walked through the house scanning shelves for possible hidden gold.

"See anything?" asked Angus.

"Not yet, but we'd better lock up anyway. We can check the barn for more molds another day."

35

Neil Giles lived for golf. He studied weather forecasts in Anderson and surrounding areas to ensure maximum days of play. During the winter months, he took as many trips as his wife would allow to warmer climates with open courses. In between times, he watched golf events on television. When the local course was closed and travel wasn't an option, and the sports channel offered only inferior sports, Neil sat and sulked. Tiring of his gloomy attitude, his wife would hand him his car keys, open the front door and invite him to find somewhere else to mope.

Neil leased a premium garage at the country club, an expense his wife gladly paid to keep him out of the house and out of her hair. Premium garages allowed room for a car and a golf cart. Hardwired overhead heating and a private bathroom made the space almost livable. Most premium lessees stored ATVs and other summertime paraphernalia in the extra space, locking the door, and abandoning the club until the next season rolled around. Neil used his extra space for a couch, mini-fridge, microwave oven, television set, and poker table for occasional guests.

Flipping through the keys on his ring, searching for the one to unlock the entry door to his garage, Neil heard a strange noise coming from the garage next door. He held the keys tight to stop the jingle and listened closely. Nothing.

Probably the wind moaning through the eaves, he thought, unlocking the door and escaping into his lair.

Sitting on the couch, deciding whether or not to call friends for a day of poker and beer, Neil heard thumps against the wall adjoining the garage next door.

Weird.

With visions of a wayward raccoon causing mayhem and destruction, Neil held his ear to the wall. Definite thumps. He went outside and held his ear close to the adjoining garage door, listening for animal sounds. Patience was the key. A moan easily mistaken for wind in the eaves came from inside.

Do raccoons moan?

Neil first considered calling the man who leased the garage in question and then remembered he'd attended the man's funeral early in the fall. Without a wife or other significant other in the picture, the lease would have gone back to the club.

He walked around to the front of the club in search of someone in charge, trying to remember the name of the woman who managed things.

Audrey? Alicia? Something with an A.

An empty parking lot and lack of lights in the building told him the place was deserted.

Weighing his options between calling the sheriff's office and animal control, Neil chose animal control. Problem was, he had no idea the number for animal control. Rick Jones, Anderson's only animal control officer, wasn't a golfer so Neil didn't have him in his contact list. On his wife's insistence, he did have the number for the sheriff's office.

You never know when you'll have an emergency!

He could hear his wife's nagging voice in his ear and decided he wouldn't tell her about this particular instance.

"Sheriff's office," said Travis when he answered the phone.

"Hey, Travis, this is Neil Giles. I think there's a raccoon in a garage out here at the golf course. Do you have Rick Jones's number handy?"

"Sure," he read a number off his desktop phone list.

"Anything important?" asked Angus, looking up from the work desk.

"Nothing animal control can't handle."

ALWAYS AT THE ready for animal emergencies, Rick kept his truck filled with necessary supplies. All he had to do was jump in and go when a call came through. It didn't take him long to arrive at the golf course and drive around to the rear. He found Neil Giles waiting, ear to door, by one of the garages.

Rick climbed out of his truck and walked over to Neil.

"Listen," said Neil, motioning toward the garage door.

Ear to door, Rick said, "That's not any raccoon sound I've ever heard before. . . unless it's injured."

"The way it's thumping around in there, it could be."

Rick tried the entry door. "It's locked."

"Yeah, can't you break in?"

"Uh . . . no."

"Not even for an injured animal?"

"No. Sorry. That rule only applies to law enforcement and people."

"Hmmm. Okay. Wha'd'ya' think we should do?"

"Who has a key?"

"The club manager, but I can't remember her name."

Short on patience in normal circumstances, Rick headed toward his truck. "Tell you what, you figure out how to get in there and call me back."

"No, wait. I'll call the sheriff. He'll know what to do."

Neil pulled up the number for the sheriff's office as Rick watched and waited from his truck.

"Sheriff's office," answered Travis.

"Hey, Travis, this is Neil Giles again. Do you know who manages the country club and how to get ahold of her?"

"Hold on. I'll ask Peter."

Remembering the slip of paper with Anne and Craig's numbers, Peter checked his coat pocket and handed the paper to Travis.

Travis relayed the information to Neil.

"Thanks, Travis."

Neil punched in Anne's number and waited. No answer. He shrugged and opened his hands in an 'I don't know' gesture toward Rick who put his truck into gear and headed out.

Not many things could peak Neil's interest outside of golf season, but an injured raccoon trapped in his neighbor's garage beat moping on the couch. Since his skills didn't lean in the handy man direction, Neil mentally ran down his list of poker buddies and landed on Eddie. Eddie, the bartender at Rustler's Roost.

Didn't he used to be in a biker gang?

If he wasn't, he knew someone who was. Neil punched in the number for his buddy Eddie and gave him a rundown of the problem.

"SO, WHOSE GARAGE is this again?" asked Eddie, lock picks at the ready, but always hesitant to run afoul of law enforcement.

"Nobody's at the moment. Remember Bill the Butcher? Worst barber in town about a hundred years ago?"

"Yeah. Didn't he die?"

"Last fall. Heck of a buffet after the funeral. They even had shrimp."

"So, who has the key?"

"The club manager, but I can't get ahold of her. If there's an injured animal in there, we don't want it to die and stink up the place."

"Good point," said Eddie. He opened a small cloth pouch, selected two small metal tools, and began his picking process. In minutes, the entry door lock popped open.

Eddie and Neil looked at each other. "Flip to go in first?" asked Neil.

"Sure." Eddie stowed his pick kit and took a quarter out of his pocket. "Call it."

"Tails."

"Dang," said Eddie. "Heads." He cracked the door open and then stopped. "Wait a minute. We didn't say if winning was going in first or getting to stay out."

"Didn't think of that. Okay, you won, it's your choice."

"In that case, you go in first."

"Dang." Neil pushed the door another inch, waiting for an angry ball of fur to come flying out. When nothing happened, he gave another push and they both stepped to the side.

An eerie groan and a thump echoed from the edge of the room.

"Is it me or did that sound human?" asked Eddie.

Spooked, Neil nodded and craned his neck to see along the thin shaft of light allowed in by the door. "Do you have a flashlight?" he asked.

"In the truck." Eddie left to fetch the light. "You're still first," he said, handing it to Neil.

"What if it attacks? Do you have a bat or something?"

Eddie paused, thinking. "Will a crowbar work?"

"Even better."

Eddie fetched the crowbar and stood behind Neil at the door.

"Don't whack me with that," said Neil.

Flashlight on wide beam, Neil eased into the room and around the door in the direction of the noise.

He stopped short. A man wrapped tight in a fetal position lay against the wall on a greasy blue tarp. Occasionally, the man would spasm, knocking a foot against the wall, followed by a pain-filled moan.

Shaking himself out of his shock, Neil ran toward the body, yelling back over his shoulder to Eddie, "Call somebody!"

Accustomed—with his job at the Roost—to calling for ambulances and the sheriff, Eddie had the numbers on the top of his contact list.

"He's still alive," said Neil, stating the obvious when Eddie joined him next to the man.

"Do you know this guy?" asked Eddie.

"Yeah, Tony Celares. Not a serious golfer."

"Scooch over," said Eddie, searching his brain for first aid knowledge. "Can you turn on the heat?"

Neil jogged to the door and flipped the switch for the heater. "Done."

"Good. Now go outside and wait for the ambulance. Close the door so we can get the room heated."

Finding no bleeding wounds or broken bones, Eddie did his best to comfort Tony while he listened for approaching sirens.

⚬⚬⬦⚬⚬

"NOW, TELL ME again how you two happened to find Mr. Celares," said Peter, as the ambulance took Tony away to the hospital.

Eddie and Neil, giddy with their heroic rescue, competed for story time and attention. Peter listened patiently, picking out the important tidbits and filing away the rest for later.

"Neil . . . when was the last time you were out here?"

He thought. "At least three weeks ago. The wife and I just got back from a trip to Arizona visiting the kids."

"Did you notice anything unusual last time you were out here? Any activity in the garage where Tony was found?"

"Not that I remember. Someone must have come and cleaned old Bill's stuff out after he died, but I wasn't around when that was happening."

"Anything to add, Eddie?"

"Nope. I don't hang out here . . . are we in trouble for picking that lock?"

"I don't think anyone will have an issue with that. You two are free to go, but I'll expect you to be available if I have any other questions."

Eddie saluted and Neil said, "Aye, aye, Captain," as they hurried home to tell their tale.

Peter stood in the doorway of the now lit garage and eyed the blue SUV style car parked on the other side of the room. Something prodded at his memory. Walking around the car, he took down the license plate number, and put in a call to the sheriff's office.

"Hey, Travis," he said when the call was answered, "can you run a plate for me?" He rattled off the number.

"Sure, hold on."

Peter could hear the click clack of Travis's keyboard.

"Is it a blue Buick?" asked Travis.

"Sure is," said Peter.

"That's our APB car," said Travis. "That's Susan Celares's car."

"One mystery solved. Now where's Susan?"

Peter finished the call. He closed and locked the door before he left. It was an easy pick.

36

"Is he going to make it?" asked Peter when Dr. Hamm ducked past the curtain covering the emergency room cubicle.

"I would say his chances are good. He's suffering from dehydration and hypothermia. My main concern was internal bleeding from the head injury, but the CT scan was clear. His thick head of hair cushioned the blow. We won't know how severe his concussion is until he regains consciousness."

"We found quite a lot of blood in his house. Could it be his?"

"Definitely. Scalp wounds are notorious bleeders. The scalp is home to a significant number of vessels."

"How long before I can question him?"

Dr. Hamm shrugged. "First he has to wake up. We'll go from there."

"Will you let me know as soon as that happens?"

"Will do."

Contemplating police protection for Tony as a witness, but short on personnel, Peter stopped at the nurses' station and spoke to the duty nurse. "He's to have absolutely no visitors. If someone tries to go in, holler as loud as you can."

Her eyes widened. "Yes, Sheriff. I'll watch him like a hawk!"

⬥

"DOES ANYONE HAVE an address for Anne at the country club?" asked Peter after several attempts to call the number she had given him earlier.

"What's her last name?" asked Travis.

"No idea. Can you get me that, too?"

"Sure, Boss."

Travis easily found the phone number for the country club, but the phone rang several times and went to voice mail. No need for anyone at the front desk during the winter and no events on the horizon. He tried to think of who would know Anne and have her last name and home address.

"Hey, Boss," he said. "Wasn't she at that church potluck?"

"Good thinking, Travis. Yes, she was. I'll bet Linda knows how to find her. I'll give her a call."

Peter picked up his phone and punched in Linda's number.

"Hey, Peter, what's up? Are you calling to make reservations for dinner tonight?"

Peter laughed, "I won't say no to that, but actually, I need help with an investigation."

"Right up my alley. What can I do?"

"Do you have a last name, address, and working phone number for Anne who manages the country club?'

"Sure do. Hold on, she'll be in the church directory."

Peter listened as Linda laid down the phone and rustled through what sounded like a large stack of papers.

"Here it is!" she said after several minutes. "Crighton is her last name, by the way. Anne Crighton." She rattled off a number.

Peter compared the phone number Anne had written on the slip of paper. An errant pen stroke made a five look like an eight on the original note. "No wonder the number didn't work. Did you find an address?"

Linda rattled off an address on the edge of town, close to the country club. "Everything okay with Anne?"

"I hope so," Peter explained about finding Tony locked in a garage at the country club. "Anne's not answering her phone and with her being manager of the club . . ."

"Oh, wow! You think someone abducted Anne, too?"

"Let's just say, I'd feel better if I knew she was safe."

"Any sign of Susan?"

"Not yet. Do you know if Anne has family nearby? Does she live alone?"

"Her husband died a few years ago. Cancer. Her kids all live out of state."

"Okay. Thanks, Linda. I appreciate it."

Peter disconnected and punched in the correct number for Anne. Still no answer. He grabbed his coat and whistled to Zack. "I'm going over to Anne's house, Travis. After finding Tony . . . I'm afraid we may have another victim."

SET BACK FROM the road in a cottonwood grove, Anne's house had a lived-in air. Multicolored Christmas lights wrapped around a fir tree in the yard, reflected on the snow. Icicle lights twinkled from along the eaves. Tire tracks cut groves up the driveway to an attached garage.

Peter pulled up to the curb and hesitated, dreading what might be inside.

"Stay here, Zack," he said as he opened his door. "We can't risk you walking over evidence."

The sidewalk hadn't been shoveled since the last snowfall and there weren't tracks to disturb so Peter waded through the snow to the front door. He pressed the doorbell, and heard a Christmas tune jingle throughout the house. Listening carefully and watching for movement at the windows, Peter waited a reasonable amount of time before he walked around the house and peeked into a garage window. The two-car garage was empty of vehicles. He breathed a sigh of relief. Anne was away somewhere, maybe out of town visiting relatives, and turned her phone off so she could enjoy the visit.

That's what he told himself, but his nagging gut said something was wrong. He walked back to the front door, tried the knob, and found it unlocked. Like many countryfolk, Anne would only lock her door if she was going away for an extended period.

Peter pushed the door open and called into the silence, "Anne? This is Sheriff Elliott doing a welfare check."

Silence. The front door opened directly into a living room. Peter walked in slowly. Remembering the pool of blood in Tony and Susan's house, he watched where he stepped. A magazine left open on the coffee table and a blanket tossed on the couch attested to recent occupation. How long had it been since Peter had seen her last? A day? Two? He walked through the rest of the house. A used coffee cup sat in the kitchen sink and a bowl of apples and bananas sat on the counter. Everything said Anne wasn't planning on being away for a long time. With a three-bedroom, two-bathroom ranch style layout, it didn't take Peter long to do a quick walk through of the rest of the house. He found a door going out and stepped down into the garage. Typical storage boxes and summertime lawn care equipment lined the edges. A bike hung from a hook on the wall. Nothing out of the ordinary. Nothing out of line.

Peter left the house, making sure to close the door firmly, and went back to his vehicle. Everything was as it should be and, yet, something wasn't right.

Not far from the country club, he drove over and found the parking lot empty. Going around to the rear by the garages, he found that area deserted as well.

Two women still missing, he thought. *They found Tony in a garage. What are the chances we'll find Anne and Susan held captive in other garages?*

Peter went back to Anne's house and let himself in, announcing his arrival at the door on the off-chance Anne had arrived home in the short time since he'd left. He made his way to the rear of the house and found the bedroom used by Anne. A flannel night gown lay at the foot of the bed. Peter slipped it into an evidence bag, hurried to his vehicle, and drove to the club. He parked at the end of the row of premium garages.

"You're up," he said as he let Zack out of his kennel compartment and snapped on his trailing harness and lead.

Peter took the nightgown out of the evidence bag and let Zack have a long sniff, "Find, Zack."

Zack wandered along the row of garages, walking through the parking lot to the rear door of the clubhouse, and back to the garages. He followed a trail around to the front of the clubhouse and Anne's reserved parking spot. Just as Susan's scent was embedded in every area of her house, as club manager Anne would have been in and out of the club, parking lots, and garages multiple times. Peter needed Zack to find the most recent scent trail. He took the nightgown out of the evidence bag and let Zack have another long sniff, this time unhooking his harness and lead and letting him roam free.

While Zack inspected every nook and cranny, Peter began at the garage where Tony had been found and walked along the line, looking for signs of activity. Most were padlocked and deserted, waiting for spring and the next golf season.

A deep bark startled Peter out of his thoughts. Zack scratched and growled at the entry door of a garage at the end of the row. Anne.

Peter ran to Zack. A quick twist to the knob confirmed the door was locked. Ear to the door, he listened for sound and was met with only silence. A single set of tire tracks went into the garage. The car had entered and stayed.

Peter took a deep breath and considered. The door was solid steel with a steel frame. Kicking it in was not the best option. Besides, Zack could be barking at a pack rat. Still . . .

Under his seat in his vehicle, Peter had an assortment of lock picking options. He retrieved the case, pulled on a pair of nitrile gloves, and chose two tools to begin the process of applying tension, and raking pins. Zack sat and watched.

Pins set and lock released, Peter opened the door, and peered into the dark room. Taking the flashlight from his duty vest and pointing it into the darkness, it revealed a battered green Subaru. Like the others, the garage also allowed space for a golf cart and all the paraphernalia involved in the sport, but this garage was empty other than the car. Trying the car door, he found it locked. He shone his light into the front and then the back seat of the car. No bodies.

"Is this Anne's car, Zack?" asked Peter as he pulled his phone out and punched in the number to the sheriff's office.

Zack sat and grinned. *I need to teach him to talk.*

"Hey, Boss," said Travis.

"Hey, could you to run a plate," he rattled off the number and waited.

"Anne Crighton," said Travis a moment later. "Green Subaru?"

"Yeah. Thanks, Travis."

"Anne's car is here, but she's not," Peter said to Zack. He looked toward the clubhouse. "Time to do some snooping."

37

PETER TRIED THE clubhouse door, expecting it to be locked, and was surprised when it swung open. A split-level entry gave the choice of going downstairs to a closed door labeled 'storage' or upstairs to the main room and offices. Peter briefly considered the best place for hiding a body would be in the storage room. Zack made the choice for him by giving a quick bark and heading up the stairs.

Sunlight shone through picture windows looking out onto the parking lot and golf course. Plastic tubs of Christmas ornaments lined the walls, ready for storage. The bottom third of an artificial Christmas tree stood in the center of the room, its top lying next to a cardboard storage box already containing the middle section. A smattering of tinsel left on branches twinkled in the light. Garland drooped from the ceiling. Whatever had taken Anne away had left the job unfinished.

Sun and glitter couldn't distract from the unmistakable stench of decaying flesh. Peter walked around the tree and there she was, Susan Celares, warmer in death than she was in life.

One eye, clouded in death, stared into the branches of the tree. A clear glass icicle ornament protruded from the other. A trail of dried blood trickled down the cheek, marring an otherwise perfectly powdered face.

Peter called into the sheriff's office.

"Hey, Boss," said Travis.

"Hey, Travis. I'm still at the country club. I found Susan Celares."

"Alive?"

"Nope. Are Helen and Angus around?"

"Angus is here writing up a report. Helen's on traffic duty."

"Send them both over and alert the ambulance for transport. I need Helen to process this crime scene and Tony's from this morning. Anne Crighton is still missing. I'm thinking we need to search the entire area."

"Got it, Boss."

Peter knelt next to Susan and studied her wound.

No doubt about the cause of death with this one, he thought.

Model slim in life, Susan's face showed signs of bloating. A greenish tinge crawled up her neck and on to the sides of her face. How long had she been here? Two or three days at least. He thought of his visit with Anne several days earlier.

Zack growled. A glass ornament, set in motion by the toe of a shoe, skittered past Peter's foot.

"Oops," said a familiar voice. "I must have dropped that one."

Peter turned to find Anne Crighton pointing a gun at his head.

"You should have let it go, Sheriff. No one will miss Susan Celares."

"I can't turn my back on murder, Anne."

The rumble of vehicle motors and the squelch of tires on snow alerted Peter to the arrival of his deputies.

"You can't gun us all down, Anne, besides, chances are that prop gun hasn't been fired since the guys put on the Battle of the Little Big Horn re-enactment down at the fairgrounds."

Anne blinked rapidly, but she kept the gun pointed at Peter. "Your deputies don't know that."

Two sets of boots thumped up the stairs, Helen and Angus chatting about a recent arrest.

As they turned the corner, Peter said, "Prop gun."

Anne screamed with rage and threw the gun at Peter. He ducked. It flew over his head and bounced off the wall.

Angus tackled Anne, took her to the ground, and held her down while Helen snapped on the cuffs.

"Put her in my vehicle, Angus," said Peter.

⚬⚬⚬⚬⚬⚬

DRIVING THROUGH TOWN, Peter glanced at his prisoner in the rear-view mirror. Untamed gray hair pointed in all directions. A stray strand of Christmas garland hung off one curl. Anne sat quietly, gazing out the window with an eerie smile of self-satisfaction on her face.

At the courthouse, Peter, per protocol, parked in the rear. He let Zack out of his kennel and Anne out of her seat, and led them up the back stairway. Anne followed along peacefully, chatting about the Christmas gala and how it had gone off without a hitch. Peter's skin crawled as he realized the woman chatting was the Anne he knew superficially. An unrepentant murderer lay under the surface.

"Cell's ready," said Travis when they walked in.

With a deputy in house, Peter would have put her in his office, but he didn't know how Travis would handle things if Anne flipped out.

"Let's put her in the cell up here," said Peter. "It's cozier."

Travis unlocked a cell door and Peter led Anne to the cot.

"What can I get for you, Anne? Tea or coffee?"

Anne smiled, "I would kill for a good cup of coffee." She giggled. "Not literally of course."

Peter released the handcuffs. Travis came in with coffee and a plate of decorated gingerbread cookies. He unfolded a TV style tray and set Anne's snack in front of her. Peter smiled. Travis had a double dose of kindness in his heart. Zack stood close to the cell door, unable to relax until Travis and Peter were safely on the outside of the bars.

Peter motioned for Travis to stay close as a witness and recited Anne's Miranda rights.

"So, tell me about Susan," he began. "How did her body come to be lying behind the Christmas tree?"

Anne took a sip of her coffee. "Not bad for a sheriff's office."

"Susan," said Peter. "Tell me about Susan."

"Oh, all right. Why can't you let things go? She was lying there because that's where she fell. With having to take down all the gala decorations by myself, I didn't have time to bring her out to the dumpster."

Travis audibly cringed.

"Can you tell me how she died?"

"It happened so fast; I don't remember the particulars."

"Try."

Anne thought for a moment. "I was standing on the ladder taking ornaments off the tree . . . those glass icicles were a gift from the mayor so I take special care with them." She sipped her coffee and took a bite of cookie, crumbs dusting her dirty sweatshirt. "Wow! These are delicious. Did you make them, Travis?"

"No. Linda Elliott. She brought them in this morning."

"She's so sweet," said Anne.

Peter cleared his throat. "You were telling us about Susan . . ."

"Horrid woman. It was such a nice day and I was enjoying the quiet, and then there she comes . . . stomping up the steps in a snit."

"What was she upset about?"

"I wasn't working fast enough. All the storage boxes should be color-coded. Did I send out the thank-you notes for gala donations. Typical Susan stuff."

"How did that make you feel?"

"Well . . . mad. I had all I was going to take from her, that's for sure."

"What did you do?"

"I told her I knew about her and Craig Schlepp plotting to sell that gold. I told her if she didn't give me a cut, I would tell Tony."

"What did she do?"

"Laughed in my face. Said I didn't know what I was talking about. Said she was going to have the board fire me for listening to private conversations."

"I'll bet that made you even madder."

"It sure did. I took that icicle and shoved it right through her eye."

"And she died."

"Well, of course, she did, but it wasn't anything she didn't deserve." Anne glanced at Peter and then over at Travis. "She brought it on herself. I'm surprised someone didn't take her out before this." She laughed, "You almost caught me, Sheriff. Coming in and asking if I knew where Susan was and her body lying right there under the tree."

"Did you consider reporting this."

"Susan dying?"

"Yes."

"No, I panicked."

"Because you killed Susan?"

"That? No. Because Susan was dead and she was my main connection to the gold."

"The gold?"

"Yeah." Anne hung her head in mock shame. "I didn't tell you the whole truth about Susan and Craig Schlepp. I knew perfectly well what they were arguing about. The vent system is old in that building and when I'm in the storeroom downstairs, I can hear everything that goes on in the office. I was down there going through Christmas decorations and heard the whole thing."

"Tell me about the gold."

Anne leaned forward. "Susan had a bag of gold coins. She wanted Craig to help her sell them. She tried to lie about it at first, but eventually fessed up that the coins belonged to her in-laws, Frank and Alice."

"How did Susan get them?"

"That story kept changing. Whether she stole them from Frank and Alice or from that Patty Giannetti woman, doesn't matter. She still stole them . . . and her walking around with her nose in the air. At least I never stole anything."

"Back to the day you killed Susan. What day was that?"

Anne thought. "Let's see. What day is it today? Well, doesn't matter. It was the day after the gala. The DAY after, and she expected me to have the decorations packed away and the thank-you notes sent."

"You said you panicked when you realized Susan was dead."

"Yes, because of the gold. You see, I deserve that gold."

"You do?"

"After all the years of putting up with Susan Celares and the rest of those snobs . . . and them not paying me enough to put anything away. I'm a tired old woman, Sheriff. I need that gold so I can retire."

"What did you do after you murdered Susan?"

"I had to find the gold, so I took her car—"

"You took Susan's car?"

"Yeah, I found her keys in her pocket . . . with house keys. So, I took her car, drove to her house and parked it in the garage so nobody could stop me from searching the house."

"Did you find the gold?"

"No. I went into the house, but then I heard the garage door going up and knew Tony was home. I grabbed the first thing I could find to use for a weapon."

"A bottle of wine."

"Yeah, it was sitting on a table in the hall in a gift basket."

"You hid around the corner, waited for Tony to walk in, and whacked him over the head."

"Yeah," she laughed, "he went down like a sack of potatoes. He bled a lot too. I was afraid I killed him at first, but he started moaning."

"Then you dragged him down the hall and out the back door?"

"First, I had to drive Susan's car around to the alley and back it into the yard. That was a little scary. I didn't want to get stuck in the snow."

"Did you lift Tony into the back of the car all by yourself?"

She lifted her arms and flexed her muscles. "Sure. Carrying heavy boxes up and down the stairs at the country club makes me stronger than I look."

"Then you drove Susan's car back to the club and parked it in the garage."

"And left Tony on that mat." She scowled. "I kept giving him chances to tell me where he hid the gold, but he kept playing dumb. I hope he enjoyed freezing to death like his parents."

"He's not dead."

"What?!"

"He's in the hospital. We found him in time."

"Did he say where he hid the gold?"

"No. Tell me about Frank and Alice."

"Frank and Alice Celares? Tony's parents?"

"Yeah, tell me about how they died."

"People say they were tied up and froze to death."

"People say?" asked Peter, confused. "That's what happened. Did you mean for them to freeze to death?"

"Me? I didn't have anything to do with that, but it was a good idea. A lot less messy than shooting someone . . . or stabbing them with an icicle."

With that she dissolved into hysterical laughter.

Travis and Peter looked at each other in bewilderment.

"I sure wasn't expecting that," said Travis.

"Me neither." Peter stood and moved his chair back to the table. "Call Missoula and arrange for transport and a psych evaluation. She's sliding fast down the slippery slope of reality."

Peter contemplated Susan Celares and Anne Crighton. Elegant and polished Susan so different from dowdy Anne, yet both convinced gold would make them happy.

38

"Can you imagine how much these are worth," said Peter when Angus and Helen showed him the bins of solid gold trophies.

"Enough that we can't keep them sitting out here in the open," said Angus.

"They won't fit in the evidence safe," said Peter. "Let's lock them in a cell, and put the key in the safe."

"Dr. Hamm on the phone for you, Boss," said Travis from his desk.

"Forward it to my office."

"He's awake and talking," said Dr. Hamm when Peter answered the phone.

"Thanks, Doc." Peter grabbed his coat and walked into the outer office. "I'm going over to the hospital, Travis. Tony's awake."

Peter walked over to the work table and found the newspaper articles from Patty and Jerry's car. "Can Zack stay here with you? They frown on dogs in the emergency room."

"Sure, Boss." Travis smiled and opened a drawer with special treats he kept for just such occasions.

Peter parked in the back of the hospital and used the rear door. Anytime he could avoid curious questions or gossip from the front desk, all the better. Upgraded from critical, Tony was moved into a private observation room. Both arms had IV drips connected, but his eyes were open and he was doing his best to eat through a tray of Jell-O and soup.

"He woke up starving, but we didn't want to feed him too much, too fast," said Dr. Hamm, sitting at the bedside. "I haven't told him any of the particulars yet."

"All I had was a granola bar and a couple drinks of water after I was abducted," said Tony, voice raspy. "How long was I there?"

"Four or five days," said Peter.

"Well . . . I'll leave you two to talk." Dr. Hamm stood and motioned Peter to follow him out the door. "His parents' bodies are thawed enough to autopsy. I'll let you know what I find out."

"Thanks, Doc." Peter went back into the room, sat in the doc's vacated chair, and leaned in to question Tony.

"Can you tell me what happened on the day you were abducted?"

"The last thing I remember is coming home and walking through the front door. I called to Susan and then everything went black. When I woke up, I was in the back of a car. When we stopped, I heard a garage door open and we drove in. Then I was dragged out of the car and tossed on the floor."

He got a panicked look on his face. "Susan. Where's Susan? Did you find her? Is she okay?"

"Tony," said Peter. "We did find Susan. I'm sorry, she didn't make it."

Tony swallowed hard and tears filled his eyes. "You . . . you mean . . ."

"She was dead when we found her. There was nothing we could do."

"I don't understand why this is happening."

"Do you know who abducted you?"

"The voice sounded familiar. It was a woman, but I never did figure out who it was."

"Do you know Anne Crighton?"

"Anne Crighton?" He thought for a minute. "The manager of the country club? Yeah. That could have been her. I've probably heard her talking at the club dozens of times, but don't recall her myself . . . she abducted me . . . us . . . why? . . . why would she do that?"

"Tony, did your parents ever mention gold to you?"

"That woman . . . Anne . . . kept asking me about 'the loot' and 'the gold'." He looked at Peter. "My parents? My dad was a school bus driver. We lived in an old farm house. If they had gold, I sure never heard about it." Sudden awareness crossed his face. "Did she kill my parents?"

"She says she didn't. Since she admits to killing Susan and abducting you, I'm inclined to believe her."

"You don't know yet who killed my parents?"

"No, sorry."

They both turned their heads at a knock at the door.

"Hey, Ross," rasped Tony. "Am I in need of a lawyer?"

Ross Robertson, in his seventies, physically fit and mentally sharp, practiced about any kind of law not covered by the local public defenders or prosecuting attorney. Hardly a family in town hadn't used his services and they all trusted him completely.

"Am I interrupting?" asked Ross, directing his question to Peter.

"Not at all. Tony probably needs a break from me badgering him."

"Please stay, though. We may need your guidance." Ross pulled a chair over to Tony's bed. "Tony, your parents had a past, a history they chose not to tell you about. They had your best interests in mind and I agreed with them."

He opened his jacket, removed a security envelope from his pocket, and handed it to Tony. "I was instructed to give this letter to you upon their passing. They shared the letter with me before the envelope was sealed so I'm aware of the contents. It should answer many of your questions."

Hands shaking, Tony took the envelope, pried the flap open, and removed a single sheet of lined notebook paper. Both sides of the paper were covered in dainty script.

Tony read the note, stared into space, glanced from Ross to Peter, and reread the note. "This is incredible."

"Incredible, but true," said Ross. "After they came to me and told me their story, I researched the history, including contacts in New Jersey law enforcement. I told them I was researching for a book so they wouldn't be suspicious. It's all true."

Tony handed the letter to Peter.

Dearest Tony-

After years of struggling with the decision, we decided the best time for you to know about our past was after we were gone.

Your father and I grew up in a working-class neighborhood in New Jersey. Unfortunately, mafia family infiltrated the neighborhood and took control of many of the businesses. We learned to keep our eyes down, our ears shut, and mind our own business.

Soon after your father and I were married, your father was pulled aside and informed that he would be the driver for the mafia boss, no questions asked. He knew better than to say no, and drove the boss and his colleagues to the airport and waited while cargo was loaded. The cargo was gold. On the way back, the car was ambushed by another mafia family and a gunfight ensued. Everyone involved except your father was killed.

He ran to the nearest pay phone and called me. I grabbed my purse and our car and met him at the site of the shootout. We transferred the gold into our car and drove as fast and far away from New Jersey as we could get. This meant leaving our families forever, but we were afraid of what the mob family would do to your father if we stayed.

This is how we ended up in Anderson, Montana. Through the years, although we lived a frugal lifestyle, we let the gold support us. Sending you to the expensive school in the east was our only extravagance. We had a story ready if anyone asked about the money, but no one ever did.

We learned how to melt and mold gold using the old forge in the barn. The original twenty gold bars have all been melted down and sold or transformed into something else.

This is where you will find gold:

1. *We always keep a bag of gold coins in the bottom drawer of the file cabinet to sell when we needed cash.*
2. *Bags of gold coins and bars in old paint cans in the shed.*
3. *The bowling trophies in your bedroom.*
4. *The bookends we gave you for college graduation.*
5. *The candlesticks we gave you and Susan as a wedding present.*

This is your inheritance. Please use it wisely.

We love you,
Mom and Dad

"I can't believe this," said Tony, still in shock.

Peter took the newspaper articles out of his pocket and handed them to Tony. "Here's a little more proof. Jerry Giannetti is the son of the mobster who pulled your dad aside to drive. He and Patty came here looking for the gold."

Tony read the articles. "Susan said she caught Patty going through Mom and Dad's files and sent her away. Patty must have been looking for the gold."

"Did Susan say anything about finding gold herself?" asked Peter.

"Susan? No." He looked at Peter. "Did she?"

"Either Patty or Susan found a bag of gold coins. Susan ended up with it. She was trying to get Craig Schlepp from the country club to sell it for her."

"Oh, Susan," said Tony, tears welling in his eyes. "She always wanted to be rich and she had a fortune in gold hidden all around her." He gave a bitter laugh. "You know those candlesticks? The ones my parents gave us for a wedding present?"

Ross and Peter nodded.

"Susan hated them. She said they looked cheap. She donated them to Goodwill."

39

S ITTING AT HIS desk with dead end solutions to Frank and Alice's murder spinning through his head, Peter was happy for an interruption.

"I've found something interesting," said Dr. Hamm on the phone. "You might want to come over and have a look."

Waiting at the door to the morgue, Dr. Hamm handed him a small container of medicinal vapor rub. "This'll help cut the smell."

Frank and Alice lay side by side on autopsy tables in the middle of the room. Dr. Hamm motioned Peter over to Alice's table and lifted a wrist. "See the slight pink lines around the wrist here?"

Peter looked closely. "Yeah."

"I think that's a handprint. Like the murderer grabbed her hard around the wrist when she was being tied up and forced to sit in the chair. She froze to death too fast for it to fully bruise, but slow enough to leave a mark."

"Could there be fingerprints?"

"It's worth a try."

"Did you find marks on the other wrist?"

"No, just this one."

Peter considered his options. He'd never taken a print off a corpse and this could be a one-shot deal. He didn't want to mess it up. He took his phone out and punched in Clementine Smith's number.

"Hey, Peter. Do you have a mystery for me to solve?"

"As a matter of fact . . . I'm over at the morgue. Have you ever dusted for fingerprints on a corpse? Is that even a thing?"

"How exciting. I have several ideas."

"This could be our one shot at the murderer. We can't mess it up."

"No worries. I've got this."

◆◆◆◆◆◆◆◆

USUALLY IN DRESSES and heels, Clem clumped down the ramp to the morgue in tall boots, wool pants, and a bright pink parka. Behind her she pulled supplies in a rolling case.

She waved away the offered vapor rub "Four decades on the ranch . . . I've smelled it all." Slipping off her heavy coat, she hung it on a hook by the door. Seeing the two bodies, she said, "Which one is going to give away the murderer?"

Dr. Hamm led her to Alice and showed her the suspicious wrist marks.

"I think you're right, Doc. When you turn the wrist over, I can see a faint outline of the thumb and three middle fingers."

"Do you think you can lift the prints?" asked Peter.

"The first trick will be exposing the prints. Our complications are the cold and wet." She leaned closer to the body. "See the condensation from her being in the refrigerator?"

Peter and Dr. Hamm leaned closer, looking for beads of wet.

Clem turned, bent down, and flipped open the clasps on her supply case. "Fortunately, I have a solution." She pulled out an ordinary white plastic hair dryer. "Where can I plug this in?"

Dr. Hamm showed her a plug-in on the side of the table.

As Clem waved warm air back and forth across Alice's wrist, she explained the procedure. "According to literature, magnetic powder works the best on old prints, but the surface needs to be warm and dry. The hair dryer is a simple fix. When I'm positive the site is suitable, I'll dust with powder as usual, photograph the prints in case the lift doesn't go well, and then try lifting the prints with tape."

After several minutes, Clem leaned over the corpse looking for moisture. She felt the skin above the possible print site.

"All set," she said as she unplugged the dryer and rolled up the cord.

She stowed the dryer and rooted around in her case until she found a container of black magnetic powder and a pen-like wand.

Peter took a deep breath and held it as he watched Clem pour a small amount of powder into a plastic dish. Suspended over the dish, the wand lifted a feathery clump of powder onto its magnetic end.

"Breathe, Peter. You're making me nervous," said Clem.

She brought the wand over, took a deep breath herself, and gently touched the powder onto Alice's wrist.

Peter and Dr. Hamm leaned closer, watching.

Dr. Hamm grinned, Peter said, "Yes!" and Clem breathed a sigh of relief when the powder first revealed the shapes of three fingers and a thumb and then defined ridges of prints.

Clem brought the wand over to the dish and released the magnet, dropping leftover powder back into the dish. She then waved the clean wand carefully over Alice's wrist to remove excess powder and released that into the dish.

Digging in her case, Clem took out a camera. She took several pictures of the fingerprints, making sure each clearly showed the print detail before moving on to her next step.

"These prints may not lift as well as we hope," she said. "But we have the pictures and that'll be enough for identification."

Clem took lift tape and print cards out of her case. She tore off a section of tape, lowered it onto the prints, and lifted. Next, she applied the tape to the print card.

Studying the card, she got a puzzled look on her face. "Hmmm," she said.

"Everything okay?" asked Peter.

"Oh, yes. These lifted much better than I expected."

"We have booking prints for Patty and Jerry Giannetti and all the prints from the Celareses' house. Let's hope something matches."

Clem packed her case and pulled on her coat. "I'll let you know as soon as I find something."

⚬━⚬━●━⚬━●━⚬

IN THE BACK corner of the sheriff's office, wedged between the long worktable and an antique oak filing cabinet, an equally old door led to a dark narrow stairway. The top of the stairs opened into a spacious room, bright and clean, with windows on three sides. This was Clem's investigation room. Work counters and modern forensics equipment filled the room. Fingerprints were processed, film developed, and evidence analyzed.

In a drawer under a state-of-the art fuming chamber, Clem had a binder of every fingerprint from every piece of evidence, from every case she had ever worked. Next to the prints, she documented the case number, the type of cyanoacrylate or super glue she used in the fuming chamber, as well as temperature, humidity level, and fuming time. A chart in the back of the binder showed the best way to program the chamber depending on what type of material the print needed to be lifted from.

Opening the binder, Clem stared at the most recent print she had fumed. Holding the print card containing prints from Alice Celares's wrist next to the one in the book, she knew her hunch to be true. A distinctive circular scar on the thumb print on Alice's wrist exactly matched the thumb print from Angela Brown's broken cup handle.

40

"ANGELA BROWN?" ASKED Peter. "Are you sure?"

"If that was her cup handle," said Clem, "there's a distinctive scar on the thumb that matches the prints from Alice Celares's wrist. Also, the fingerprints from Alice's wrist match the partials from the church door note."

Peter stuck his head out his office door and saw Angus sitting at the work table writing a report. "Angus, come in here."

Angus jumped up. "Sure, Peter. What's going on."

"Let me see your thumbs."

"My thumbs?" Angus lifted his hands splayed open toward Peter. "Why do you need to see my thumbs?"

Peter studied the thumbs for a moment. "No scars. Good."

At Angus's confused look, he said, "The broken coffee cup handle you brought in . . . Angela Brown was using that cup? Nobody else?"

Angus thought for a minute. "I remember her taking that cup and the one she gave me out of the cupboard. They were different colors so they couldn't have been mixed up. She was drinking coffee out of it before she dropped it."

"And she lives alone?"

"As far as I know."

"We need to bring her in. The fingerprints we took off Alice Celares's wrist match Angela's cup and the church note."

"Angela murdered the Celareses?" asked Helen, hearing the tail end of the conversation as she came in from a call.

"I thought we had her alibied," said Angus. "The tracks in the snow were from her going to the church for AA."

"Tracks in the snow?" asked Helen. "But the murders happened before the snow. Anything that happened after the snow is insignificant."

"Oh, dang," said Angus. "I broke the number one rule."

"Assuming?" asked Helen.

"Yeah, I assumed Angela's AA meeting covered her lie about not going anywhere. She never said she didn't go anywhere else."

"Dr. Hamm said there's no way of telling when they were murdered," said Peter. "They had undigested breakfast food in their stomachs, but it could have been any day after they called in that grocery order and that happened before that snow storm."

He grabbed his coat and whistled to Zack. Angus retrieved his coat from a hook by the door and they ran down the courthouse steps to the parking lot.

⚬━●━◆◆━●━⚬

SOMEONE HAD CLEARED Angela Brown's lane since the last time Angus had been out to her place. Warmer weather brought the animals out from their shelters. Chickens pecked in patches of earth uncovered by melted snow. Llamas basked in the sun.

"How do you want to go about this?" asked Angus.

"First, we look at her thumbs. Clem showed me the scar on the prints. If Angela has one to match, we have enough to bring her in."

As usual, the mismatched pack of dogs heard Peter's Explorer coming up the drive and ran out to greet their visitors. Angus, accustomed to the dogs, assured Peter they were harmless.

"That says something coming from you," said Peter, stepping out of the vehicle. Angus exited on his side as Angela came to the door.

"The sheriff and his deputy," she said, lacking her usual spirit. "It must be serious."

She led Peter and Angus into the kitchen. "I don't suppose you want coffee," she said.

"Not today," said Peter. "I need to see your thumbs."

"My thumbs," said Angela, surprised.

She held up her hands, splayed forward like Angus had when asked. Peter looked closely. Her right thumb had a distinctive circular scar.

"Interesting scar."

Angela looked at her thumb and then at Peter. "I've had it since I was a kid. I don't remember how I got it."

"We found a thumb print with that same scar on Alice Celares's wrist. Can you tell us how it got there?"

Dropping into a kitchen chair, Angela put her face in her hands.

Peter and Angus waited in silence for her to speak.

"I didn't mean for them to die," she said, pulling her hands away.

"But you admit you tied them to chairs and left them to freeze?" asked Peter.

"Yes, but you don't understand. It was . . . well, I wasn't thinking right." She looked at Angus, willing him to step in and help her. "I was drinking and drunk . . . and so depressed. And we had that cold spell. All I could think of was Asher down under that cold ground. My poor baby . . . so cold. I wanted Frank Celares to be cold too."

"I drove to his house. He and Alice were sitting there eating breakfast all warm and happy. They let me in before they saw the shotgun. After that it was easy. I made them move their chairs into the living room and sit while I zip tied their hands. Alice wouldn't hold her wrists tight together so I had to hold them until the ties were fastened. I wasn't thinking about bruises or fingerprints."

"And you left the door hanging open so they would freeze?"

"I wanted Frank to feel as cold as Asher. I didn't mean for them to die, Sheriff. Honest. When I heard they froze to death . . ." She sat and shook her head in sorrow. "That's when I called Linda Elliott for help with the drinking. She brought me to AA."

"So why did you ransack the Celareses' house?" asked Angus.

"What? I didn't ransack the house," said Angela bewildered. "I tied them up and left. Everything was fine then."

"One more mystery to solve," said Peter. "We have to bring you in. Do you have someone who can take care of the animals?"

Angela made a few phone calls and said goodbye to her dogs. "Without Asher, none of this matters anyway," she said as Peter led her to his vehicle.

⊸•◦•◆•◦•⊷

MEEK AND DEFEATED, Angela allowed Peter and Angus to book her into jail without struggle. He alerted Travis to the new prisoner and arranged for meal accommodations added to those already arranged for Jerry and Patty Giannetti.

One question still worried Angus's brain.

"Hey, Peter," he asked, "any thoughts on who ransacked the house? It made sense when we thought it was an angry murderer threatening them, but Angela had no reason to do that."

"What are the chances Patty had something to do with it?"

"That's my guess. She's not going to admit it though."

"Jerry might know. Let's have another chat with him."

Angus went to the cells and brought Jerry to Peter's office.

"I'm ready to get out of here. What do you need to know?" asked Jerry.

"You and Patty are off the hook for the murders."

"For sure? You found the guy who whacked them?"

"Girl, actually, but yeah, we did, so you're off the hook for that. What do you know about the mess in the house?"

"Yeah, that was Patty. She was mad about Susan getting her kicked out of the house, especially since Susan took the bag of gold . . ."

"So, you admit Patty found a bag of gold," said Peter.

"Yeah, what of it. That Susan witch took it, not Patty."

"Where did she find the bag?"

"In a file cabinet."

"So, Patty left that day, but went back?"

"Yeah, she found out where the witch lived and parked over by the house. When she knew everyone was home there, she drove up to Alice's house to try and talk her way back in. She can put on the charm when she wants to."

"But you never went up to the house?"

"Nope," he grinned. "I'm clean."

"You let Patty do the dirty work and take the fall if she gets caught."

He shrugged. "It works."

"Go on. Patty went to the house . . ."

"They were already stiffs when she got up there. She was mad because she thought someone else made off with the gold."

"Mad enough to tear the place apart?"

"When Patty gets mad, she gets mad. Kind of likes messing up places."

"Good enough. Angus, take him back to his cell."

"Wait a minute," said Jerry. "I told you what you wanted to know. Let me out a' here."

"No, sorry. We still have you on felony theft."

"But Patty took all that stuff."

"It was found in your car, which makes you an accessory."

Face flushed, Jerry jumped to his feet, ready to throw himself over Peter's desk. He stumbled, clutched at his chest, and gasped.

Peter stood and steadied Jerry, helping him back to his chair. "Angus, call the ambulance."

WITH ANGELA TUCKED in for the night and Jerry under observation at the hospital, Peter decided against going home and cooking for himself. He punched Linda's number into his phone.

"Is that offer for dinner still open?" he asked.

"Always," laughed Linda. "I have a big pot of chili bubbling on the stove."

"Great! I'll be there in a jiffy."

<hr>

SITTING AROUND LINDA and Paul's cozy kitchen table, Peter waited until he had the first bowl of chili in his belly before he told them the good news.

"We found the church money," he said while buttering a chunk of corn bread and tossing it to Zack.

"What?!" said Linda. "That's wonderful! Where? How? Tell us the details!"

"We found it in Patty and Jerry Giannetti's car along with Nadine's paintings and a bunch of other stuff. No guarantee the cash is all there, but she hadn't tried to cash the checks. That's how we knew it was church money."

"Hallelujah!" said Paul. "And praise God, Nadine has her retirement back. That loss would have been heartbreaking."

"We also found Tony Celares."

"Alive?" asked Linda.

"Alive and expected to fully recover." He told them about the garages at the country club.

"And Susan?"

Peter hesitated. "We found her. Murdered."

"Oh, dear," said Paul. "His parents and now his wife."

"Who and how?" asked Linda.

"Anne Crighton." Peter relayed the story.

"Anne," said Linda. "Wow. She always seemed so normal."

"I expect they'll send her to a psych ward somewhere. We'll see what the experts say."

Linda and Paul, dinner forgotten, focused their attention on Peter.

"Any other breakthroughs?" asked Linda.

"We also found Frank and Alice's murderer," said Peter between bites of chili. "Angela Brown."

This time the reaction was more somber.

"Angela? But she has an alibi. She was here at an AA meeting."

"The murder happened before that. We didn't investigate her as well as we should have, giving her the excuse of a grieving mother battling with alcohol."

"I imagine," observed Paul, "It's hard at times to stay neutral during investigations when it's people you know."

"What next?" asked Linda.

"Patty and Jerry . . . a.k.a. Priscilla and Gerry with a G, are charged with felony theft and assault. They'll go through the legal system, as will Anne and Angela.

Oh . . . I almost forgot, but keep this to yourselves. Tony has enough to deal with without moochers hitting him up for donations. Angus and Helen found the gold."

Peter relayed the story of the golden statues.

"The loss of family and freedom in exchange for revenge and wealth. Will any of them think it worth the risk?" mused Paul.

"Tony is the innocent in the whole thing and the only one around to feel regret," observed Peter. "Patty and Jerry would have been caught for theft eventually, regardless of their plot against Frank and Alice, and Angela is too deep in mourning for Asher to care about her own situation."

"Will Tony be expected to return the gold?" asked Linda.

"According to Ross, the statute of limitations on the original theft expired decades ago. Any proof of where the gold bars came from melted away in that forge. A court wouldn't touch the case. Reporting the gold is a can of worms none of us want to open, especially Tony Celares."

"Oh," said Linda, "I almost forgot. We heard from Bill and Kathy Edwards."

"And I completely forgot about them with everything else going on," said Peter. "I guess they're cleared for the murder. Where are they?"

"Bill checked Kathy into a treatment center in Billings for depression and grief counseling. She was too embarrassed to tell anyone and didn't want to take the risk of going anywhere closer and running into someone they knew."

"How's she doing?"

"Much better. She feels horrible about the way she treated Frank and Alice, but understands she wasn't thinking straight. Frank and Alice aren't around to make amends so she called and apologized to Tony."

"That's great. Does Tom know?"

"Oh, yeah. He's taking it easy on Kathy, but gave Bill a good chewing out for putting him through all that worry and stress."

41

A WEEK LATER, FEET on desk and phone in hand, Peter chatted with instructor Adam Henry of the Helena Police Academy.

"So, the victim, Tony Celares, wants to host a community education event training people how to escape zip ties and car trunks."

"That sounds great," said Adam. "It's actually possible if the victim knows the tricks and doesn't panic."

"Uh . . ." said Peter, "Helen will probably be there."

Adam hesitated and cleared his throat. "Does she know I'll be the instructor?"

"She doesn't know about the event. I wanted to talk to you first."

"Does she say anything about me?"

"Not a word."

"I don't know what happened, Peter. Everything was great and then I offered to take her on a winter break to a sunny beach somewhere. She's been avoiding me ever since."

"Hmmm. Weird. Do you mind if I run this past my sister-in-law? Completely confidential, of course. Maybe she can shed light on the situation."

"That'd be great. Thanks, Peter. It's been eating me up thinking I offended her."

"No problem. I'll let you know and keep you posted on possible dates for that community day."

Peter disconnected and punched in Linda's number.

"Hey, Peter. What's up?"

He explained Adam's dilemma with Helen.

"Oh, Peter. You know Helen struggles with her weight. There's no way she wants to go to a beach with a guy she's dating."

"Why not?"

"And let him see her body, belly rolls and all, shoved into a swimming suit?"

"A girl thing?"

"Oh, yeah."

"What should I tell him to do?"

"Call and tell her he won't be able to go on vacation . . . too much to do at the office or something. Then tell her he misses her and ask her out to dinner and a movie . . . or whatever they usually do on dates."

"Thanks, Linda."

Peter disconnected, called Adam, and passed on the information. As he was saying his goodbyes to Adam, Clem knocked at his door.

"Hey, Clem. Thanks for all your help clearing up those murders."

"All in a day's work." She settled in a comfy chair in front of his desk and cleared her throat. "I went to Missoula and talked to the manager of the restaurant where your parents ate before they were murdered."

Peter tensed, ready for bad news.

"He remembers that night in detail," said Clem. "With his memories and the other witnesses listed in the murder file, I think it's worth pursuing."

"What do we have that the police didn't have back then?"

"DNA, the silent witness. At the time of your parents' murder, DNA testing wasn't available."

"Was there possible DNA evidence?"

"Strong evidence, not just possible. According to the eye witness, the mugger was wearing a black face covering. A black ski mask was found on the path in the woods. Considering it was summer, chances are better than not that the mask belonged to the mugger."

"That's, well, that's excellent. Wow! Thanks, Clem."

"I need your help with something, though."

"Sure, anything I can do."

"I'm a civilian, Peter. In order to investigate and have access to the ski mask and any other evidence, I need authority."

"Oh, of course." Peter opened his top desk drawer, pulled out a deputy badge, and slid it across his desk. "Welcome to the force."

Clem pinned the badge to her shirt and grinned. *I can do this!*

<hr>

EARLY THE FOLLOWING spring—ground thawed and road to the cemetery open for travel—Lee Garnet oversaw setting grave stones for Asher Brown and Carl Revell. Later that week, Paul Elliott led a community memorial service for the deceased Celareses and the three boys killed in the bus accident.

Tony Celares stood at the edge of the crowd, feeling like an outsider. After losing his wife and parents, and inheriting riches of dubious origins, Tony's relationship with the rest of Anderson had become awkward. He longed for the days of mediocrity; ordinary parents, ho-hum job, comfortable house, dissatisfied wife. Most folks struggled to move past the pity stage. Many, not knowing what to say or how to act, avoided him entirely. Others insisted on discussing the tragedy ad nauseum until he avoided them. Occasionally, Tony crossed paths with someone who continued to blame his father for the bus accident.

With twisted logic, they transferred their hate to Tony. He heard whispered opinions that Susan's greed was the catalyst to her own death. *She had it coming,* the voices sanctimoniously declared. Opportunists did their best to relieve him of his fortune and others judged him for keeping it. The bank respectfully asked Tony to resign as his family scandal and the gold seekers lining up outside his office disrupted business.

Tony studied the crowd. Angela Brown, serving time in Montana State Prison for her part in the deaths of Frank and Alice, was notably absent. Bill and Kathy Edwards, scandal-free, stood front and center flanked by Tom and Judy and surrounded by friends.

A choking sob caught Tony's attention. He turned to find June Revell half hidden in the branches of a Ponderosa Pine. Her purple hair had faded to a soft shade of pink. Black slacks replaced the jeans and a long-sleeved blouse covered most of her tattoos. Up until now, whether in denial or under pressure from her boyfriend, Doug Kromer, June failed to acknowledge the death of her son Carl. Whatever the reasons, Tony wasn't going to let her mourn alone. He walked to her hiding spot and gave her a full bear hug. Taking her arm, he led her to the front of the crowd where she could stand by Carl's grave and grieve openly.

Paul's message focused on forgiveness and unity. Peter stood with his deputies at the edge of the crowd, listening to the message of hope, and prayed for a long season of peace.

Thank you for
reading Nefarious Intent!

Have you considered leaving
a review? Reviews help me
spread the word and help other
readers decide if they want
to enjoy the book, too.

Please scan the QR code
below and let me know
what you think! :)

-Kit

GET YOUR FREE EBOOK

Join the citizens of Anderson in *Mountain Tales,* an ever-growing collection of short stories about past and present mysteries.

SIGN UP AT KITKARSON.COM

BOOK 5 IS HERE

Warm spring days take a chilling turn when local rancher, Seth Geary, discovers the mutilated body of his ranch hand alongside the carcasses of several slaughtered cows.

FIND IT AT KITKARSON.COM/BOOKS

www.ingramcontent.com/pod-product-compliance
Lightning Source LLC
Chambersburg PA
CBHW022024310726
48972CB00006B/1797